BEYOND

THE SEA

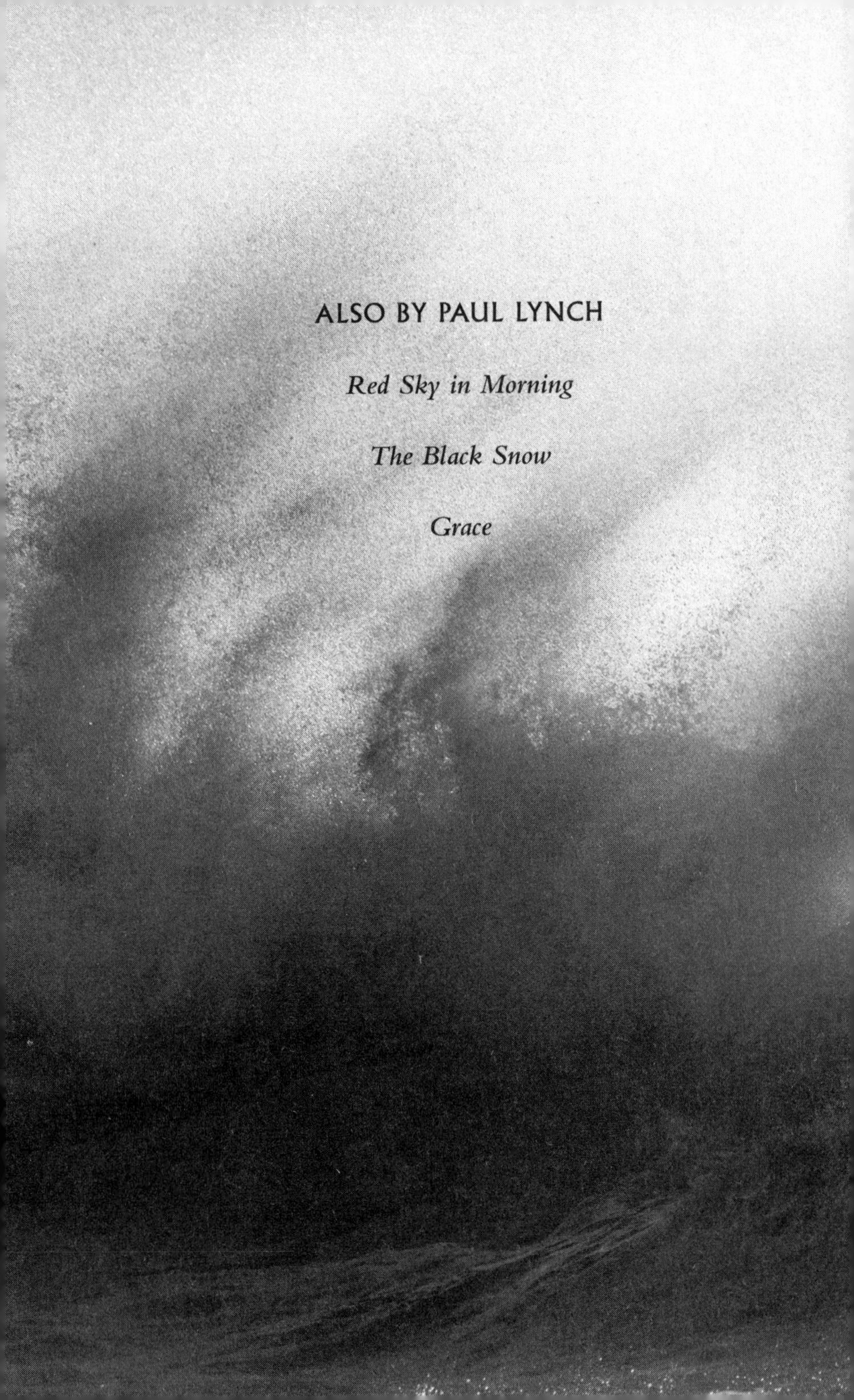

ALSO BY PAUL LYNCH

Red Sky in Morning

The Black Snow

Grace

BEYOND THE SEA

PAUL LYNCH

Farrar, Straus and Giroux

New York

Farrar, Straus and Giroux
120 Broadway, New York 10271

Library of Congress Cataloging-in-Publication Data
Names: Lynch, Paul, 1977– author.
Title: Beyond the sea / Paul Lynch.
Description: First American edition. | New York : Farrar, Straus and Giroux,
2020. | "Originally published in 2019 by Oneworld, Great Britain, the
Republic of Ireland, and Australia"—Title page verso. | Summary: "The
haunting story of two men stranded at sea pushing against their physical
and mental limits to stay alive" —Provided by publisher.
Identifiers: LCCN 2019046743 | ISBN 9780374112431 (hardcover)
Subjects: GSAFD: Suspense fiction.
Classification: LCC PR6112.Y534 B49 2020 | DDC 823/.92—dc23
LC record available at https://lccn.loc.gov/2019046743

Our books may be purchased in bulk for promotional, educational, or business
use. Please contact your local bookseller or the Macmillan Corporate and
Premium Sales Department at 1-800-221-7945, extension 5442, or by
e-mail at MacmillanSpecialMarkets@macmillan.com.

www.fsgbooks.com
www.twitter.com/fsgbooks • www.facebook.com/fsgbooks

1 3 5 7 9 10 8 6 4 2

For my son Elliot
and my father Pat,
mariner turned coastguard

Who knows if life be death or death be life?

—*Euripides*

It is not a dream of storm weather that follows Bolivar into the town, but words overheard last night, perhaps in Gabriela's bar, that give him the feeling now of a dream. He thinks, it might have been the chatter of Alexis or José Luis – who knows, they are such troublemakers. And yet this feeling of dream persists. It is the feeling of a world once known, but forgotten, asking from over the sea.

His sandalled feet follow the road over the crumbling bridge. Past the empty beachside cabanas. Past where the nesting sea turtles scallop the beach. His eyes seeking out beyond the lagoon but his sight is drawn towards the shore. An oilcan lies washed up and surrounding it a glittering of dead *popocha* fish. He fixes his baseball cap and walks onto the beach.

He thinks, it is just a dozen or so, but still. Even the beggars won't touch them. There is a sickness in the rivers that no one will ever explain.

He studies the indigo dawn for trouble. He studies the clouds and the wind. That the ocean has a hue is a lie among men. He cannot remember who said this. For the sea contains all colour and in that way everything is within it. This might be true, who knows what you hear.

The plastic white seats at Rosa's café lean like drunk sleepers to their tables. He slaps at a net full of beach balls hanging from the *palapa* roof. Damnit, he says. Angel is not waiting. He kicks a seat past the beach screen and the back of the seat cracks when he sits. His hands rest on the spill of his gut as he studies them. Such hands are too big, perhaps, and he has often thought this. A forearm for a wrist. A thigh for an arm. Shoulders for a neck. But what else do you expect for a fisherman?

He turns his head and shouts, Rosa!

From here he can see the panga boat he thinks of as his own, alone and high up on the beach. The white hull with *Camille* painted in turquoise. Angel is not there either. He can see the ghosts of two men, his earlier self and Angel last night and how they sat in that panga, moon-drawn effigies of fishermen drinking beer amidst the bodiless shouting and the gaunt light thrown by the bars on the strip.

He calls again for Rosa, can hear that crazy Alexander at his singing, the old man's voice a glass-bright tremolo. He leans until he can see him on a cooling box of some undetermined long-ago colour. The flashing of nails as he repairs sea-worn nets. Each day Bolivar tries not to listen, yet still he listens, for such songs evoke in him feelings he cannot explain. Sometimes a feeling like guilt. Sometimes a feeling of being alive long ago, as though he had lived the life of another, and what are you supposed to make of such a thing?

Loose sand rolls across the matting. He puts a finger to his nose and gouts snot. Rosa!

It is the Virgin of Guadalupe on her high shelf who watches Bolivar as though he were an apparition gliding through the hanging beads of the door. There is Rosa asleep on a hammock, she is always asleep. He reaches for the remote control and turns the TV on to a game from the night before.

Rosa! he says. Have you seen Angel?

The woman stirs with a vexed sound. With pendulous feet she swings out of the hammock and stands in the half-light tying up her hair. Just her eyes he can see as if they can draw what there is of the light towards them. He blinks at her twice and an old part of his mind thinks of her as some witch in the dark until she rolls up the screen and her body finds its expression. His eyes following the light as it falls upon her loose-shirted abdomen, upon her glossed hands and thighs. His eyes prizing her the way a man prizes a woman.

Has Angel not turned up yet, Rosa?

That box of limes, Bolivar. Did you bring them? I asked you last night.

He is either here or not here. I have just a few limes to take with me on the boat.

How Rosa seems to sigh in everything she does. Her body is sadness bending to the fridge. She pulls from it two beer bottles, the movement of hinging upward is a weariness that does not belong to a woman as young as this. She uncaps both bottles without looking, rests a stare upon some faraway thought out past the lagoon.

Bolivar holds her with a look as he takes a long drink. A goal sounds on the TV and he leans for a moment out the beaded door, returns wiping his mouth with his wrist.

You will not believe it, he says. Remember that great fish kill last year? I just saw some *popocha* washed up dead on the beach.

Rosa studies him a moment.

She says, some man came round here looking for you last night.

What man?

I don't know. He said he was going to cut off your ears.

It is him.

Who?

I have done something stupid. But I will fix it quick.

He watches the way her right eye pinches when she drinks. Watches this cool brick room where she lives. A hammock and two palm-wood chairs and a humming box refrigerator. The trace odour of sweat. Her clothes hung upon nails.

He reaches out to touch her wrist but Rosa pulls back, the words passing unthought out his mouth.

Some day, Rosa, you should marry me. I am only a fisherman, it is true. But I will pay off your TV. Maybe even buy you a jeep. I will buy you some furniture for your clothes. I'll give you all the limes you want.

Rosa stares at his sun-browned feet, the taped plastic sandals, the plump spread toes. The big toe on his left foot missing a toenail.

Bolivar turns his foot inward as she looks at him.

She sighs. I have so much to do, Bolivar. Those limes. I have to go.

They listen to Alexander laughing to himself.

Bolivar turns towards the door and the old man begins again to sing.

That fool, he says. Whoever knows what nonsense he sings.

Rosa says, those songs are sung to the bones of the dead.

Bolivar pulls at a piece of wall plaster.

This place is falling apart, Rosa. One of these days the wind and the sea will carry you away.

Rosa shrugs. I do not think today will be the day.

Arturo! Bossman! Bolivar steps into Arturo's office with its front facing onto the beach. He takes a long inhale. The freshening breeze carries within it the faint rot of the sea. He shouts again and fixes his cap. A two-way radio crackles then fades into faraway static. Arturo is where he always is, he thinks. Asleep in his room with that woman or watching TV or maybe he is at Gabriela's already having a drink, grouching about who is shortening his pockets.

He walks into the back yard and sees Little Arturo sitting on the steps. The boy a direct image of the father or what he may once have been. The heavy-browed face that is a sign of the man to come.

Where is the bossman? I need him quick.

The boy's eyes rest vacantly upon Bolivar. He shrugs and continues to thumb at a phone.

Is he in or not?

Above them a door opens and a head appears with hair askew. Arturo moves barefoot down the cement stairway and meets Bolivar with a flat-faced look. Bolivar studies him. Arturo is wearing the same grey vest and red shorts he wears every day. For sure, he sleeps in his clothes, those clothes have become skin.

Arturo says, come here, Porky, I want to show you something.

Bolivar follows Arturo and stands before a peacock-toned 4x4 jeep. Arturo points a finger at it.

Look at this, Porky. Tell me, who would do such a thing?

Bolivar follows the man's finger and hunches down. He runs his hand along a scratch keyed deep into the paintwork. What travels into his skin is a feeling of guilt and yet he is sure he did not do this. He searches his mind and meets a feeling it was Angel. He stands up and sighs, fixes his cap, pulls at the waistband of his shorts.

Looks to me like some drunk, maybe. Or just some kid. There are lots of kids causing trouble. Tell me, Arturo, bossman, have you seen Angel? He has not showed up.

Arturo turns upon Bolivar with an examining look. Then he closes his eyes and when they open again they rest mournfully on the jeep.

I cannot believe it, Porky. Nothing in this world stays new. I thought you had gone out yesterday. You should be coming back in today. Why didn't you go out with the others?

Ring him.

Ring who?

Angel.

What for?

I need to go out but how can I go without Angel? I do not fish with anybody else.

Arturo exhales deeply and turns towards the sea's ashen hue. Then he turns and stares at the man before him.

Listen to me, Bolivar. There is a storm coming from the north-east. The bulletin is out. Look at the beach. Most of the boats are pulled up. The rest are coming back in.

That is not true, Arturo. I watched three boats go out. Memo's boat and two others.

Yes. Memo is crazy like you, Porky.

Ring Angel.

Look, Bolivar. Nobody is sending you out.

Ring him.

Why?

Bolivar winces, begins to pull at an ear.

Look, I need to make some money quick.

Why don't you ring him?

Bolivar shrugs. My phone is dead. It is broken. I have no credit. That last woman took it when she ran off. Look, I am only a fisherman.

Arturo pulls a phone from his back pocket and squints as he dials. He stares at the jeep then shakes his head and hangs up, dials another number.

Hey, Skinny, I have Porky here with a spare hand down his pants. Have you seen Angel? His phone is dead. Go knock at his door.

Bolivar watches the man on the phone, watches the image of the man as expressed in the jeep's burnish.

7

The man become shimmer, a reflection of will that is the devouring soul within him. He watches Arturo's face, how of late it has begun to deepen in colour as if exhibiting some shade of stagnating blood, the blood pitching towards some final dark colour. The flesh is coming loose over the bones, he thinks. It is happening as you watch.

Arturo's eyes are lost in a stare as he listens, his eyes seeing not directly the beach nor the lagoon but beyond, past the surfers and shrimp fishermen, past the hazed and unmet horizon.

Arturo nods and hangs up.

Angel is not at home, Porky.

Maybe he is sick or dead or something. You need to find me somebody quick. And make sure they are good.

I will find you somebody, Porky. But why can't you go out like everyone else? You come here and I give you a cabin and you used to fish but now you drink the days away instead. You believe in nothing. You care about nothing other than yourself.

How is this true?

Prove to me it isn't true.

Listen, Arturo, bossman. What difference does it make when I go out, if it is this time or that? OK, so I did not go out at sunrise today like the others. But I do what I like. I know all the best places. I go out farther than anyone else. They go out thirty miles, forty. They are like children. I go out a hundred miles if I have to. I go to the reaches of the earth. I have no limit.

Porky. There is a storm coming that is really going to blow.

Bolivar studies the sky.

It looks fine to me.

Bolivar straightens up from the boat to see Arturo stepping towards him with a long-haired youth. He hurries them along with his eyes then looks to the sea. He leans out and pulls into the boat a refuse sack full of ice. From the verge of his sight he studies the youth. It is in the youth's slack walk, he thinks. In those loose arms and wrists. That stooped build. He is an insect from the mangroves, for sure.

He leans out of the boat and spits onto the beach.

As they near the boat Bolivar stares directly at the youth until the youth lowers his gaze.

Then Bolivar turns to Arturo. What is this? he says.

He picks up the sack and pours the ice into a cooling box six foot long that rests in the centre of the boat.

This is your new shipmate, Porky. Say hello, Hector.

Bolivar steps around the cooler and stands in the stern facing Arturo.

Find me somebody else, bossman. This kid knows nothing about fishing.

He turns and watches the youth's collapsing expression, the stumbling tongue, how fright alights the eyes and channels the limbs until the youth stands with his hands unsure.

Bolivar balls the empty sack and throws it onto the beach.

Arturo says, go easy, Porky. Hector here has plenty of experience. Isn't that right, Hector?

He puts a hand upon the boy's arm and squeezes.

Hector's tongue struggles to life.

I— I worked the lagoon on Papa's boat last year. I worked the motor. Back and forth along— Look. I couldn't care less.

Arturo jerks Hector's arm.

Hector says, OK. How much is he paying?

Arturo nods at the boy and smiles.

His father is a cousin of Ernesto who fishes with my brother. I found him just now on the beach. You can give him a loan of some gloves, or whatever.

Bolivar pretends to consider this for a moment but he is studying instead the jungled hill behind the town. He has never really noticed it. How it sits like a great wave woven to stillness by nature. He considers this thought and finds it strange, imagines lying in bed with Rosa. Imagines having her inside the cooler, there is enough room for two in there though it would be a squeeze. But for the smell of fish it would be the best lay ever.

Bolivar folds his arms and stares at the youth.

He says, fishing the lagoon is not fishing.

Hector shrugs and shakes free of Arturo's grip and makes as though to walk off.

He says, I have other things to do.

Bolivar studies the sea where gulls whirl upon two approaching boats. He looks down and sees his two ears sliced off and lying on the sand. He turns to Arturo who has taken hold of the youth by the elbow.

OK, bossman, he says. Just this once. I have to leave quick. I'll pay him thirty.

Arturo says, forty, Porky, forty.

Bolivar bends and takes two empty petrol containers and bundles them into Hector's arms.

He says, take these to the bossman's tank and fill them. Then bring six more.

Arturo says, hey Porky, I met Daniel Paz just now. He says something happened between you two last night.

Between who?

You and Angel.

What do you mean?

He said something happened.

Nothing happened.

Something.

Nope. We drank in Rosa's and then in Gabriela's and then we drank in the boat and then I went home and maybe he kept drinking. Whoever knows with him.

So where is he?

He went to his mother's, Arturo. He forgot. He was arrested again for taking his whistle out in front of that policewoman and asking her to blow it. How do I know, Arturo? I am only a fisherman.

He walks with gloved hands staring at his feet. Down the strip road beneath the palm trees. The sound of a revving truck reaching obscurely into his thoughts. A known figure forms before him, utters some greeting and steps past. It is Daniel Paz, but Bolivar does not look up. He is thinking about the man who is looking for him. He thinks about his ears. He takes a look up over the treetops and out past the lagoon. It might be true there is a storm coming, he thinks. But it does not look like much.

Bolivar walks towards the panga carrying two buckets of sardine bait. His gaze locked upon Hector. The way the youth leans against the boat chatting into the phone, one hand loose, the small mouth laughing.

Bolivar thinks, he is still some kind of insect, for sure.

Hector watches for a moment then ends the call, begins to clear his throat.

Listen, Bolivar. I cannot go out. Daniel Paz said it is going to storm.

Bolivar laughs. What are you talking about?

Hector laughs but the laugh stops short under the eyes. Then his mouth tightens. He pulls the hair out of his eyes, meets Bolivar with a direct look, his body straightening out of its slack expression.

Bolivar lifts his hands from his hips and folds his arms so that he stands before the youth bulked and implacable. Hector's jaw tightens a moment then falls loose. He goes to speak but his eyes drop from Bolivar's face, his gaze travelling to meet a faded name-tattoo on Bolivar's forearm, then a beggar bending with a stick far up on the beach. When he speaks he is staring at the ground.

Look, he says. I cannot go even if I wanted to. I have a game later. I promised my girl I would meet her.

Bolivar loosens his arms. He slides his left foot out of his sandal, bends and rubs sand off the base of his foot, puts the sandal back on. He sees Hector noticing the nail-less toe. He takes a step closer, looks at Hector's ears.

What did I say I would pay you?

Forty.

I will give you sixty.

Hector's mouth opens and his tongue moves but no sound comes out. His hands go into his pockets. He pulls out his phone. He half-turns and pretends to thumb at it.

Then he says, you are crazy, Bolivar.

Tell me, Hector, what is a storm? It is a little windy, that is all. The sea gets a little choppy. Real fishermen are used to this type of thing. I have not yet met a storm that is the boss of me. We will go straight out and come straight back in again. No trouble. Look at this boat. It is the best boat here out of all the others. I talked to the bossman. He listens to the radio. He says, whatever this is, it will blow itself out pretty quick. It is nothing to be afraid of.

Hector's eyes swivel towards somebody walking up the beach.

Bolivar turns to see Daniel Paz and Arturo, the bossman's gaze fixed upon him. Paz laughing at some joke.

Bolivar takes a step towards Hector.

Look, he says. I will give you half my share. That is the deal I have with Angel. You cannot do better than that.

Hector's sight falls upon the two men then falls upon the boat, travels across the sea to where the daylight hangs in a flattening colour.

Bolivar watches the gaze go slack, the shoulders soften, how the hands sit restless in the pockets.

Bolivar whispers, half.

Arturo shouts, Porky!

Bolivar turns and quickly speaks.

Nothing to see here, bossman. When we get back we will party like wild animals for days. Isn't that right, Hector?

Arturo stops and studies the boat. He looks out upon the sea. Then he studies Hector and smiles.

That guy you told me about, Porky. The one who can get rid of industrial waste. My brother knows a guy with a tank of spoiled molasses he needs to get rid of.

He becomes his hands and eyes and hands and eyes become the sea. The boat cutting a path through folding ocean. He has motored the panga between shore and lagoon. Past shorebirds staved upon sandbars. Turned then directly into the wind. A low haze of sea-made light. He pulls a pre-rolled joint and a yellow lighter from his pocket. As he exhales he thinks of Rosa. Next time you will bring limes for sure.

Watching the water's endless heave that has no place of origin. Watching as Hector leans upon the gunwale trim, the youth spitting into the wind, the spittle rushing like an insect. Bolivar begins to feel it under his skin, an itching here and there that is a deepening dislike of the youth. Only now does Bolivar see what is printed on the back of the boy's sweater — a skull and crossbones.

He thinks, Arturo is having a laugh, for sure.

Bolivar stares at Hector's thin attempt at a goatee beard. Then he lets out a pirate's roar.

Hector turns around with a puzzled look, meets the toothy disarray of Bolivar's nut-brown grin.

*

At fourteen miles on the GPS he passes two shore-bound boats. Knows one of them for Ovidio's boat, a stripe of yellow upon white. The way Ovidio stands with his foot upon the gunwale, his finger and thumb loosening a whistle. Then Ovidio shouts two blurry words but Bolivar stares straight ahead as though he has not seen them. Hector half-stands and waves until Bolivar picks up a sardine from the bait bucket and throws it at him.

He motors the boat blinking against fine spray. One eye upon the GPS, a thumb wiping the screen. It is this that he seeks. Farther ocean. The taste of salt on the lips. Time receding as the hair-fine shore falls away. He tries to read the sea but his gaze keeps meeting Hector. How the youth grips the gunwale while searching on his phone for a signal. When Hector asks how far left to go, Bolivar cups a hand to his ear and shrugs. He watches the youth turn away. Watches the wind pulling at the ponytail, the hair blowing this way and that, Hector tying it back into place. Bolivar takes off his baseball cap and puts on a woollen hat, hangs the cap on a hook under the seat.

When Hector turns and asks a second time, Bolivar stares at him and shrugs. It is then he sees in Hector's eyes a flashing look of anger. Bolivar turns away but holds up two tobacco-stained fingers.

Two hours more, he says.

It is quarter past five when Bolivar stops the motor.

The world falls into a vast quiet. Just the sound of the sea carrying the breeze on its back. He rests an elbow on his left knee and shakes the stiffness out of his tiller hand. Then he curls his fingers around a joint.

Hector turns with an expectant look.

Bolivar sucks upon the joint and pulls from under his seat a pair of grey rubber gloves. He throws them at Hector and releases a cloud of smoke.

Hector stares at his hands loose in the gloves.

The sun falling beyond the sea.

Bolivar says, now we begin.

Caves of dying light in the sky. Each man dissolves into the gloom as they finish baiting the hooks. Hector feeding the unhurried line hand over fist as Bolivar reverses the panga. He watches the bleach-bottle floats become dim jellyfish. He watches for the last moment of light as it meets the dark, narrows his eyes and tries to see it. He has a bet with Angel about this, some day yet I will see it, for sure, the exact moment it happens. He imagines it making a sound – a gasp or a pop. He cuts the motor and listens to the world as though met with sudden loneliness.

Bolivar flicks a butt over the trim, looks up to see the full moon obscured behind clouds. He reaches for the battery lamp and flicks it on. Then he fixes a plastic head-lamp over his woollen hat. Without a word they eat some bread and cooked liver and onions. Bolivar sprinkling a pinch of seawater on his food.

He studies Hector by lamplight. How the youth slumps over his bowl taking small bites. The mouth hanging slightly open. The jaw born short under the mouth.

He leans closer for a better look, thinks he has not really noticed this. The long face and the short jaw and how this seems to give the face an agape look.

Hector leans across to free a smoke from the roll of Bolivar's hat.

Bolivar leans back, says, you have to ask first.

Hector says, can I have a smoke, please, Porky?

Bolivar frowns and leans forward.

What did you say?

Hector says, *please*, can I have a smoke?

That is not what you said.

Bolivar blinds the youth with the lamp, watches the eyes puzzle, the light of an uncertain thought passing across the face.

Hector says, that *is* what I said.

You called me a name.

Hector swallows and studies his feet. He digs the toe of his shoe into the hull. Finally he looks at Bolivar.

Isn't that what Arturo calls you? Porky?

Bolivar fixes upon Hector a withering look that goes unseen in the dark. Hector pulls at his hands then reaches slowly into his pocket.

He says, do you like chocolate?

I have never yet met a person who does not like choc-olate. It is the one thing everybody can agree on.

Do you want some?

No.

Bolivar switches off the battery lamp and the world falls into a limitless dark. He listens to the meshings of the wind and the sea, thinks he can hear Hector chewing.

The tongue squirming the chocolate into paste against the teeth, the short jaw working.

He thinks, damnit, Angel would have brought beer.

A short while later, Hector says, it's just over a month to Christmas.

He begins to talk about the football last night, about who will win the game tomorrow, about this girl he is seeing, Lucrezia. How he spends all his money on her yet is not sure whether he likes her or not – one of her eyes is not right, it is her left eye, no, it is her right. You do not know if she is looking at you or not.

Bolivar sucks a joint to life and passes it to Hector.

He rolls another for himself.

He listens to Hector shifting about the seat.

Then, finally, he says, this is where they go.

Hector says, who?

The runners for the cartels.

Hector's voice returns pinched. Out here?

For sure. Keep the lights off just in case.

How do you know?

These are their waters. One night close by here on the GPS, Angel swore he heard a boat being shot up. Heavy weapons. This might be true or not true but I was asleep, I didn't hear anything. Victor Ortiz was out here with Pablo T one night last April when they heard screams and shouting. Let me tell you what happened. They cut their lights and sat and listened. That is definitely the sound of a boat in trouble, Victor Ortiz said. Don't go to them, Pablo T said, I have a wife and children. But Ortiz gunned the motor and began in their direction in a zigzag motion.

Pablo T beaming a strong light. His light fell upon a boat.
Then Pablo T quickly turned off the lamp. They watched
that boat in the dark and both said later they were struck
with the same feeling, that the boat they were looking at
was empty and that they were being watched by a third
boat hidden in the dark, a boat with no lights yet full of
men in hoods or balaclavas with heavy weapons trained
on them. Then Pablo T said a prayer and he turned on the
lamp and trained it on the first boat. What they saw was
an empty fishing vessel. The hull sprayed with bullets and
not a soul upon it. After that, both Victor Ortiz and Pablo
T said they would not come out this far again. Maybe
what they heard were ghosts. Or maybe what they heard
was the sound of people being fed to the sharks. That
much is probably true. What do you think, Hector? Do
you believe in ghosts?

Bolivar stretches out across the seat and pulls the cap
over his eyes.

In a skim of sleep he hears it. The maddened wind.
Tunnelling out of dark to reach another dark more true
than dream. He rolls the cap from his eyes, looks to where
the moon should be. The sea is twisting the wrong way.

This is unreal, he thinks. I cannot believe it. It has
come in the flick of an eye.

He tries to see the illumined dial of his watch. There
is a roar and then a crash as a wave strikes the boat. The
water transmitting sudden cold into the bones. Bolivar
bends out of the blow wiping brine from his eyes.

Hector screams awake.

A quickness now of things, Bolivar a liquid black towards the bow. The boat riding the dark swells. He passes Hector who has come to be on hands and knees and he roars at the youth to bail. Hector not real now but an imagined thing cowering in the boat which is also the unimagined thing – Bolivar aware for an instant of this thought as it passes through his mind, his body moving without thinking.

Without gloves he is upon the sea-cold line, fire in his hands as he hauls it. Behind him Hector is shrieking. Bolivar roars over his shoulder at the youth to bail, sees instead Hector taking hold of the battery lamp and shining it at the sky.

A world come howling from a dream.

Salt stings his eyes. I am blind, Bolivar thinks. Then he flicks on the headlamp, a steeple of light in the dark. Hand over fist he pulls in the line, hitches it to the two-headed bitt, the boat pitching downward as he gaffs a shark in the mouth and hauls it. Then he unhooks the shark and sees by lamplight into the shark's eye, is met with a fleeting unintelligible feeling of some other world. He clubs the shark on the head and throws it into the cooler.

It is miracle work and yet he moves with a feeling that something is within reach, a defined edge of his being. Already he has landed and unhooked four big fish, the line laden, the bait has done its work. Whispering to himself about Hector who is cowering in the stern, screaming and refusing to bail.

He thinks, you knew it the moment you saw him. It

was in his walk, in the way he stood, in that short little jaw of his.

He becomes aware of water touching his ankles. He turns towards Hector and shouts for him to bail but his voice is flung the wrong way. He hitches the line and walks down the boat, grabs the bailing bucket, ropes it to the underseat.

The hissing salt–spray.

Hector's shouts thrown into whisper.

Dear God, please, I don't want to die.

The sound of the wind funnelling through dark space.

How an hour becomes a life. Some distant part of Bolivar's mind speaks but he does not listen. He is busy doing the work of two men, bailing the boat and hauling the line, gaffing fish after fish, throwing them into the cooler. Soon the cooler is half-full with tuna and a few sharks.

For sure, he thinks, this is the best place yet. Just another hour or so and there will be light.

He meets the blow of each wave while Hector can be heard sobbing. Now and then the youth begins to bail but stops when hit by a wave.

It is a simple matter, Bolivar thinks. Staying alive. Doing what you are supposed to do without question. This boy is a fool, he will not listen.

He thinks, this will make for some tale back home. He will never live this down on the strip.

It is then that Bolivar turns and roars.

Come on, we are going to do this.

*

It comes in whisper. An awareness that he is working against his own feeling. Then something deep sounds in the wind. He can feel his heart shake. His mind speaks words to what he already knows as feeling. That what has been has not yet met its limit.

The boat shudders violently upward and he finds himself thrown onto his back. The boat is almost taken into the wave's mouth. He turns and can see Hector crouched and kissing a crucifix necklace. He is calling for his mother, his father, calling for God to listen.

Bolivar is caught in a tangle of line. He picks himself up and yanks a hook out of his shirt, tearing the flesh of a rib.

He stares into the face of the north-easterly gale.

There should be light now winging the west.

He thinks, there isn't time.

He grabs the line and takes the gutting knife and begins to sever it. When the line slips off the bow he turns upon Hector, pulls him in a rage by the sweater so that they are face to face. Hector's mouth opens, his eyes squeezing shut against the direct light of Bolivar's headlamp, against the dark of the storm, the crucifix falling from the mouth.

Bolivar gives him a violent shake.

Come on, he shouts. It is time to go. We can do this. I just need you to bail. We will sink if we take on any more water.

Hector is crying or perhaps he is just trying to wipe the brine out of his eyes. Then he begins to nod. He moves towards the bucket and grabs it with both hands, begins to bail as though met with a sudden rage.

Bolivar yanking the motor to life.

*

In sunless greylight Bolivar motors the boat, blinking furiously at a compass. Watching the needle teeter. Watching the rollers obscure the sky. He forges a path through each ravine, opening the throttle then slowing. Both of them bending to take the blow of each wave. For a moment Bolivar can see them on some prehistoric earth met by perpetual storm, time unravelled, no day or night, no distance to be measured. What the world once was or yet will be.

He thinks of Rosa, his mind travelling down her skin towards her hips, the long bones of her thighs. This feeling now after so many years of looking at her. To lie with her each night would be to get the pain of wanting out of the body. What you have to say to her. Yesterday I was poor but today I am rich, that is the life of the fisherman.

Bolivar roars out, that's it, keep going! In a few hours we will have a few beers—

The boat plunges then recovers and Hector whips his head up and stares at Bolivar, his face frozen by what he sees.

Bolivar rising out of his bent posture with a wide laughing mouth, a great hand spread on his thigh.

The boat mounts a mass of reaching sea. Bolivar roars at Hector to grab the gunwale but the youth continues with outflung elbows to bail. Everything on deck begins to slide – the remnants of the fishing line, their bags, the buckets and knives, Bolivar locking his feet to the hull as he screams out at Hector, the fibreglass beginning to quake. He is aware for a moment of a feeling of emptiness as a mouth of ocean opens behind them. Then the sea becomes sky. He bends his head between his legs as the panga crests the top of the wave, an enormity of iced thunder breaking upon them. He finds himself seated, his hand gripping the tiller, and in the same instant without looking he knows Hector is gone. Quickness then as he swings his sight over the side, a thought that says, let the fool go. Yet it is then without thought that he reaches out and grabs Hector by the hair. He pulls the youth towards him as the boat continues its downward pitch. He can feel the fingers coming loose as the body is pulled away from him, his arm losing reach, there is no time to do this, he thinks, let him go, he will take you with him. It is then with his left arm that he takes hold of the gaff and roars strength into the lift, pikes the youth into the boat by the hood of his sweater.

Bolivar bends under another wave, blinks the salt out of his eyes. It takes a moment to see. There is Hector stunned but alive, an animal in the moment of birth. The mouth sucking for air, the eyes swollen tight, the body sealed in mucus. He rolls onto his side and spews water, begins to move as though met for the first time with weight and breath. His hand reaching upward to grab hold of the trim.

It is then that Bolivar knows the motor is dead.

He grabs the pull-cord and yanks it. Yanks and yanks it again. The engine's powerhead is silent. He roars at it then turns and bangs it with the base of his fist. He begins again at the pull-cord.

Finally he stops and looks up.

Catches sight of a tossed bird.

He grabs the two-way radio from under the seat and shouts into it. The speaker is silent. He thumbs at the button and wipes the mouthpiece on his shirt, checks the channel and dials up the volume. He holds the radio to his ear, cannot tell if the radio is clicking or not.

He looks across and sees Hector watching him, the youth grey-skinned, the whites of the eyes rawed to the colour of blood yet carrying a look of disbelief as if what is happening now might not be if only he could wish it.

Bolivar shakes the radio then puts it down.

He shouts, maybe it ran out of juice. We had no time to recharge it. Maybe it got wet. They are never truly waterproof.

It is then the radio crackles. Bolivar thumbs the button and shouts. The radio clicks and a distant voice decays into static. He wishes it were Arturo but he knows it is not. It is probably another boat out here, no doubt Memo or one of the other boats is in trouble. He remembers what somebody once said, how a radio signal sent and never picked up can forever orbit the earth, a long-lost call of the dead.

Who knows what you hear.

He roars again into the radio but does not tell Hector what he soon knows.

That the radio is beyond use.

That they are truly on their own.

Bolivar studies the lashed sea. It is from there they will come, he thinks. Seeing in his mind men powering through the waves. Paz will volunteer. The Cruz brothers. Maybe Angel will turn on his phone. He will be the first in a boat. He will know where to find you.

He shouts to Hector and points towards the coast.

Do not worry, they will come! The Cruz brothers, for sure! They are the best of men. If they can find Angel, they will know where to find us! Only he knows where I hide out.

Hector's sorrowful, weighted eyes are the eyes of a man watching his own life from some remote place without capacity to shout warning. And yet as Bolivar shouts the head rises and the eyes narrow in alarm. He reaches and takes hold of Bolivar's arm.

He shouts, what do you mean only he knows where to find us? Do they not know where we are? Isn't there GPS or something?

Bolivar bends under a wave and Hector blurs under the wash. Then Bolivar wipes his narrowed eyes with his wrist, surveys the boat a long moment, then slides off the seat. Hector's mouth falling open as Bolivar throws the petrol cans overboard. Then he moves towards the cooler and grabs hold of a young bluefin tuna, throws it into the sea. He roars at Hector.

We are too low in the water. Quick, empty the boat.

Hector it seems cannot move. He stares in horror as Bolivar throws a shark overboard with a laugh on his face.

They will come for us, you will see! I have done this

myself for others. Many, many times. You spend a few extra days at sea then you return and cook a huge barbecue. I will buy all the drinks.

Every bone shouts for sleep. His eyes are stung shut. He forces his sight upon the perpetual dusk but there is nothing to see but the coming night. A full day spent within the storm, bailing the water out of the hull, emptying the body of strength. He has taken what remains of the line and cut it in two, tied one half to each side of the boat, let it out with the floats for ballast.

Now he rests with his eyes closed again, his head upon his arm. It is then in his mind he sees the cooler. He lifts his head and stares at it. Then he hauls himself up, roars at Hector for help.

Hector refuses to look.

Bolivar leans into the cooler's dead weight. He roars at Hector again until the youth crawls towards him. Together they lift the cooler and turn it onto its side. Bolivar climbs in and shouts for Hector to join him.

Inside the cooler the sea throws them together. Hector's elbow in Bolivar's face, Bolivar holding his head in his hands. Hector talking incessantly to God, begging for protection, asking to be spared, the hands wringing, clasping in prayer.

Bolivar meets a feeling of fate coming upon him.

He thinks, so it has come to this.

He climbs back out and bails furiously, then climbs back into the cooler. Feeling the spent arms and legs. Feeling the void of how many hours of night ahead.

Moving blind through this shrieking dark. Lying in this cooler with Hector. It is then Bolivar begins to laugh.

He thinks, for sure, he is no Rosa.

A feeling of sleep without sleeping. Or maybe sleeping without sleep. Asleep maybe and yet the body listens. The body listening with an almost seeing. The senses alert to every motion of the boat. He knows a larger vessel would have been smashed by now. Instead the panga rides each mountainous wave like an insect. Now and then he climbs out of the cooler with his body hunched, his arms bailing heavily in the dark. Seeing by the dying headlamp. A deepening sense the storm is blowing itself out. Without words he understands that the true meaning of a storm is what it reveals, how chaos describes itself, gives form to what no eye can see. What he knows now but does not tell Hector. That this north-easterly is blowing them far out. We must be a hundred miles out into the Pacific. No one will look this far.

A dream of silence. He wakes to a clear sense of things. Water lapping the boat. A still light. He inhales the cooler's in-baked smell of brine and fish. For two days and nights he has watched his life from within some dark cell of the mind. Eternity within each waiting moment. Climbing out of that dark to bail water. Snatching at sleep. Now he can hear Hector asleep with a rasp in his chest.

Bolivar climbs out of the cooler and has to pull at his stung-shut eyes.

The sun soaring over emptiness.

*

The panga is low in the water, the water in the boat sits past his ankles. The bailing bucket is still tied by the stern. Behind him Hector climbs as though broken-backed out of the cooler. His frame shrunken, his pallor grey, the under-eyes swollen and black. He cannot see yet, keeps rubbing at his eyes with his fists. Bolivar sits huddled and blinking. For a long time they do not speak.

Then Bolivar mutters something, his voice a scratched whisper. Hector tries to focus his eyes on Bolivar. He winces and continues to rub them.

Bolivar begins to knuckle the boat with amusement.

He says, this thing is indestructible.

He leans forward and points to a pomegranate bruise above Hector's left eye.

He says, what happened your head?

Then he slaps the hull and laughs loudly.

It looks like Hector is forcing the eyes to see into the laughing mouth before him, the bronzed teeth, the tongue lolling. Bolivar clapping his hands again as he stares with amazement at the cooler. Then he turns and sees in Hector's eyes the panicked look. The youth climbing to his feet, the youth turning around to take in a smooth and single plane of ocean. The world containing nothing but its perfection.

Bolivar fishes the two-way radio out of the water between his legs. He thumbs at the button, stares at the blank screen. Then he smacks it against his knee. The GPS screen is also dead. He puts the two devices on the seat and stares at their plastic shapes, the electrical life dead inside them, their buttons beyond use.

The small bilge pump is dead. He spends time quietly bailing water, Hector watching with a half-turned head, his arms long on his lap. He has become aged in posture as though looking back on a life, hateful and bent. Then he stretches his body across the seat to dry in the sun, a crimson sickled gash along the length of his ankle.

For a moment Bolivar stops bailing and studies the youth. The draped arm. The half-risen knee. The sighing mouth.

He thinks, it is something within the spirit, the spirit always against the doing thing. Here we are half-dead and still he has no use.

So many things are lost. The petrol cans, the plastic bags with food and clothing. The lines that gave ballast torn from the boat. Bolivar counts eight floats that can be used to cup water. He finds an eight-inch gutting knife and a wrench. Sees that his watch has stopped working. He pulls from under the two seats a four-foot plank used to clear debris before the propeller. There is a five-gallon container full of water. Bolivar uncaps it and takes a look in. They each measure the other's sip.

With a grunt Bolivar places the motor's cowling on the deck and bends to examine the powerhead. After a while, he shakes his head and looks up.

He says, I thought maybe there was a problem with the fuel pump or that water got into the fuel line, that is usually the issue. But I'm not sure. You could not have predicted so many things would happen at once. I just cannot believe it.

Hector turns and stares at Bolivar as he leans back, his legs and arms splayed out as though idling on the strip, the wrench on his lap, he is almost smiling. The way he leans forward to loosen something between his toes.

It is then with a shriek that Hector rushes at Bolivar, knocks him off the seat and grabs the wrench, begins with a howl to smash the motor, Bolivar lying astonished on his back. He sees an engine part spin into the air, another fall overboard. He cannot move until he hears the shout within him to move, the mind moving past disbelief to enter the body. He finds himself upon Hector. He grabs the youth by the throat and drags him, Hector releasing a sob and then a choking sound, his hand rising up as he throws the wrench overboard. Bolivar slams him onto his back, sits his weight on top of him. Then Bolivar's fury cools when he sees the spirit of the storm brought to boil in Hector's eyes. The swollen eyelids that do not blink their look of savage hatred.

Bolivar clears his throat then speaks in a low voice.

I should kill you right now.

Hector's mouth pulls a mocking smile.

You already have, Porky.

These are the longest hours. This the longest day. They sit in an imprisoning sunlight, silence massing between the two men. Bolivar leans slowly out of the cooler sucking on his tongue. A great exhaustion has spread within the body. The body pulling at the eyes resting upon the sea. Watching and watching until the sky and the ocean seem to flatten, become one thing. He closes his eyes and opens them. Soon again the sky and the ocean begin to flatten, distance falling away. Colour and space merging now into a single vertical plane.

He can feel it closing in.

He closes his eyes and tells himself, it is an illusion, a trick of the sea. He wonders why it is happening now to him. For how many years have you been a fisherman? You are not a beginner like him.

He fixes his sight upon Hector. The youth sits in a stoop by the bow with his back turned, his hands playing at something. Bolivar leans farther out of the cooler, then edges forward without sound, but Hector turns as though he can feel Bolivar's eyes upon him, his hand putting something away.

Bolivar sits and closes his eyes and listens to the ocean. When he opens his eyes he tries to teach his mind to see the ocean as it is. Sunlight wrinkled upon the water. Pilot fish scurrying the clear waters by the boat.

He lifts his eyes towards the horizon but again the waters and the sky begin to meet, his eyes now seized by what he sees – a wall of single colour closing in, a wall rising until it seems he is trapped in the bottom of a hole, a prison of single colour risen above him, towering towards infinity.

Bolivar will not watch the waters. For hours he sits in the cooler with his hand over his eyes, aghast by what he has seen. Watching the shadows crawl along the hull. Watching the dark grow complete. Then he lifts his eyes. There is the North Star. There the gibbous moon. The world again as it has always been. It is then he sees in Hector's hand the glow of his phone. The youth flicking through photos, it seems. That phone useless out here.

Bolivar slides out of the cooler, moves soft-foot towards Hector. He steps on a screw knocked loose from the motor, howls and grabs his foot. Hector stirs and turns, then stows the phone in his pocket. From his darkened corner he gives Bolivar a wary half-look.

Bolivar climbs back into the cooler with the screw in his hand. He rubs at his foot and pretends to chew at a fingernail. He rolls the screw and thinks about the wrench.

When he climbs out again he moves without breath, his back hunched, his feet silent upon the hull. Hector does not hear until too late, Bolivar reaching over the youth to grab hold of the phone, Hector turning, rising out of the seat with a hand outstretched, a sound in his throat like a sob cut short.

Bolivar says, say goodbye to your sweetheart.

A dark mouth of sea opens and closes around the phone.

They huddle together in the cooler trying to keep warm. Hector refusing to speak to Bolivar. Instead he pleads with God in urgent whispers. Again and again he shifts position, his torso turning this way and that, his knees wriggling under his chin. He is trying to scratch some place beyond reach, Bolivar pushing against him, nudging with his elbow, muttering curses under his breath.

In his mind he is sipping a beer. He runs the malt over the tongue, leans against the bar talking with Angel, the man laughing as he listens. You would not believe it. He was like a child. He didn't stop crying—

Something heavy brushes the hull.

Hector leans quickly forward.

He whispers, what was that?

Bolivar says, it's nothing. A shark, maybe. Who knows.

He notices how Hector sits very still. The listening mind riding the passing breath. The passing breath expiring unseen into the night. What the night does not reveal, an answer to give rest to the reaching mind.

Bolivar sits listening. He can hear the youth's exhaustion

drag the breath down into the body. Soon Hector is asleep. He begins to snore and Bolivar tries to sleep but cannot, the sound of Hector's breathing boring into his ear until finally he roars out and elbows the youth in the ribs.

Hector startles awake.

Hey, kid. How can you snore like this? You are not at home in your bed.

They wake into a profound indigo silence. A world without answer. Hector reaches for the water bottle. Bolivar stops him with a hand to the wrist. He points to the floats and says, pass me two cups. He pours a splash of water into each. Then he says, put a little salt in your mouth before you drink. He watches Hector as though father to the child, the way the child drinks with two hands to the cup.

Bolivar sits staring at the water bottle. He thinks, three or four days of water and then we are in trouble. He imagines how it will be when the water runs out, the very thing every sailor fears – the mind giving in to the sea's whispers. The hand dipping the cup. The water passing the lips and sating the thirst with salt to burrow the blood and deepen the thirst until you dip your cup again—

He puts some dried salt on his tongue then puts the cup to his lips, sees that Hector is watching him. He allows the water to sit in his mouth a while before swallowing.

He chews a little lip skin.

The taste of salt in the cracks of his mouth.

*

The hours grow empty and pass by. Then Hector leaps to his feet and points eastward. Over there, he shouts. Bolivar rubs his knees and climbs out, stretches his upper body. For a long time they rest their sight upon a light aircraft catching the amber sun, a spark loosened by fire. Bolivar drops his visored hand and squeezes Hector's shoulder.

He says, it is searching for us.

Hector wiggles free of the grip.

Bolivar reads the plane's unreachable distance, a stretch of sky that could be ten miles. He shouts until his voice is hoarse, his cheeks surging with blood.

Then the plane is gone.

Bolivar turns fiercely upon Hector, grabs him by the arm.

He says, what is wrong with you? Why wouldn't you wave and shout?

Hector pulls free, sits down and shrugs.

What is the point? he says. A boat this size is invisible to a plane that far away.

Bolivar begins to rub his eyes with his fists. When he lowers his eyes to the youth they are red-rubbed and bloodshot and narrowed with scorn. The eyes addressing the meatless frame with a single unblinking look. The way Hector slumps on the seat with the long hair curtaining his face. Then Bolivar puts his head in his hands and sighs.

Look, he says, I am not saying this isn't bad, but they are looking for us. We will be rescued. That is a fact. There is procedure, protocol, rules to be followed, the coastguard goes out and that plane goes out, how many times have you seen it? Arturo's men, they drop everything and keep searching. I have done this myself. Many, many times. We brought Memo and Herman back last year. Think of that. Their motor broke down just like ours. They were at sea for four days. Memo was giving out because he ran out of crackers. I am telling you, we will be on the strip by tomorrow night. Drinking beers. That girl of yours, what do you call her?

Lucrezia.

Yes, she will be waiting for you. Think of the things she will do for you then. A-ha! They will have taken measure of the wind and the current. Worked out our drift. So keep your spirits up, eh? We will figure this out. In the meantime, we can try and catch fish.

Hector's face pulls into wrinkle. He moves his hair out of his eyes, his gaze travelling throughout the panga.

He says, catch fish with what? You are such an ass, Porky.

Bolivar sees the youth's eyes lit with defiance.

Again he shakes his head.

He says, what is it always with you? Have you no spirit? Do you want us to die?

Hector puts his hands to his face and weeps. When he lifts his face he stares at Bolivar with a long and earnest look.

He says, listen, Bolivar, I am sorry about the motor.

Bolivar shrugs. It is OK, it was useless anyhow.

They fall silent. Then Bolivar rubs his hands and speaks.

I would cut off my two ears to get back soon. If I don't, that Arturo will send somebody else out with Angel. That bossman is cruel. I will be out of a job.

Hector says, I need to get back also. If I don't get back, I'll miss the play-off for the cup.

Hector awakes panicked into black night. He grips Bolivar by the wrist, then leaps with a scream out of the cooler. I am blind, he shouts. I cannot see. They are never going to find us.

Bolivar's mind passing out of some dream. He reaches after Hector, seizes the youth from behind, can feel the breath wild in Hector's lungs. The storm of thought let loose throughout the body, the blind and searching fear passing through the blood, the hands reaching for the trim, Hector trying to pull free from Bolivar.

Bolivar keeping hold of the youth till he is calm.

He stares at where the moon should be.

Look, he says. Over there. Behind that cloud. You can see the moon. It has begun to wane now. The North Star is behind that cloud. It will be bright in a couple of hours.

He persuades Hector to sit in the cooler.

He sits with the youth, listening to the wild breath giving shape to the mind inside. The mind's storm-wind and how it moves blind against the dark.

Later, when Hector is asleep, Bolivar remembers the dream from which he had woken. How he was standing before the house of his parents, asking them for something, but they stood with their backs turned.

*

These waiting days. Their reaching eyes. Watching the sea for boats. Watching the sky for rain. Watching jets pass by distant as comets. Watching a vessel of some kind for hours, the craft red-hulled, shiftless on the water. Bolivar waving and shouting into cupped hands. Hector asquint and half-standing, his hands gripping the gunwale. Then his shoulders slump. His voice falls into whisper.

It is just a piece of debris.

Later, Bolivar says, we are drifting westward, one or two knots, maybe twenty-five miles a day.

The boat carried by a current that starts and stops, spins them a little, then carries them onwards again.

They watch the east recede. The west vast and silent.

They move the cooler so that the opening faces north. Spend their days inside it hiding from the sun. Each man sitting knees-to-chin and almost naked. Each man sucking on a dry tongue. How quickly the skin grows a hard coat. The hair thickening with salt.

Hector sits glum-faced, the hands idle, the tongue licking slowly at the teeth. Bolivar sits taking the motor apart with the knife. After a long time he frees a choke link from the carburettor. I wonder if this could be made into a hook, he says. Then he fondles a spring. Maybe this will work better. Maybe it won't. For sure we will need some gut.

He watches the sun in its unvarying expression upon the sea. In the evenings he leans over the glassy waters, watching the bloom and gustings of shoals. He sees pilot fish in hornet coats. Triggerfish feeding off the hull. They snap at his bleeding fingers as he grabs at them. With a whoop he finally lobs one into the boat. The eye bulbed with an unfathomed look. His fingers bleeding onto the fish as he cuts it, the knife greedy, his fingers pulling at the flesh, his mouth pulling on the juices. Hector refuses to eat the fish raw. He says, it always makes me sick. Bolivar stares at the youth as he slowly shakes his head. He says, I've never yet met a person who doesn't like raw fish. It is the one thing everybody can agree on.

He picks up a fish eye and sucks it like a sweet, pops it between his teeth, watches Hector turn away in disgust. He places some fish on the cowling.

Maybe if I dry it a little in the sun, you will eat some?

Hector turns and watches Bolivar clean and fillet the fish, leaving the meat attached to the skin. He slices it into strips and places the meat on the cowling. Hector studies the fish with a soured mouth then shrugs.

Maybe.

Bolivar watches the world ranged in unbroken colour. Sending thought into the ocean's depths. Sending thought to meet the shadows that pass beneath – sharks, dorado, tuna. Other unnamed things. Watching a shadow great and implacable deep in the water for much of a day, as though the shadow were a refraction of his own thinking, the thoughts he will not speak. That their water is running out. That the sky signals days without end or rain. That the workings of his mind are slowing. He is having trouble keeping track of time.

He thinks, the days have only been a handful, it is true, but what was yesterday might have been today or just an hour ago. Out here time plays tricks or ceases to be time in the usual way.

Bolivar lifts his face to the sky and smiles.

It will rain soon, he says. I can feel it.

A breeze rises and Bolivar ties Hector's sweater to the rail. For a moment the wind climbs inside it, the sweater rousing full-chested to let flag a skull and crossbones. Then the sweater drops and does not rise again.

Bolivar laughs and slaps his knee.

He says, they will never believe it when they find us.

He turns then and stares at the perpetual sea.

Faint whispers of horror come upon him.

Where they are now in this ocean and its forever.

He wakes in painted light. Hears a strange *schlik schlik* behind the cooler. He shakes from his mind a dream of clear water, climbs out and sees Hector bent to the hull. The youth turns when he hears Bolivar yawning. The *schlik schlik* stops.

The air is cool and Bolivar rests his eyes upon the ocean. What moves as light could be a boat or a far-off signal or even a piece of refuse. Light resting in the water's eaves. Light golden at the morning's edges. He thinks about how in light like this he would watch the world come to be from his cabin door. He leans over the side of the boat and watches for triggerfish. He turns to speak and it is then he sees what Hector has done to the hull.

He moves towards the youth with a pointed finger.

What is this?

Hector shrugs indifferently.

Bolivar bends to see six fish-bone lines scratched into the boat. One more day and Hector will be able to scratch a line through it.

Bolivar maddens, sees the rage before him, steps into its pleasing rush. He steps before Hector's face, jabs him with a finger.

What are you doing? Hey?

Hector shrugs but does not speak.

We are not in prison.

Bolivar leans closer still.

Hey! Look at me when I talk to you. We will be rescued today or maybe tomorrow. Or the day after that at the latest. This is a fact. In the meantime, do not put another mark on my boat.

He rubs at his throat for it has hurt his voice to shout. There is no saliva in his mouth. He takes the knife and begins to scratch out the markings.

Hector stands slowly blinking. Then he sits and watches Bolivar working the knife into the hull, Bolivar cursing, turning then to see a smile resting in Hector's mouth, the smile passing.

The sun beats upon the panga. They sit in the cooler, Hector's mouth hanging open. Bolivar stares at his own hands. He closes and opens them. Slowness now has entered the body. A tightness in the mind. He closes his eyes and can see the blood congealing within the body. The thick blood slowing the fingers. He closes and opens his hands again. These hands that still seek the doing thing.

He fondles the empty five-gallon container then climbs out and places it carefully under the stern seat.

Hector sits pulling at his cheeks, the skin taut about the upper neck, the short jaw hanging as though in readiness to shout. But he is silent.

Bolivar sits back into the cooler and with a sideward glance studies the youth. The skull seems to have lengthened, he thinks. The limbs grown longer. Only a few days have passed and already he has changed.

Evening light, a jet plane prising open the distant sky.

Bolivar leans over the hull watching for small fish. He watches the shadow of a shoal pass by. Then, six feet away, a commotion in the water. He sees a dorsal fin break the surface then smoothly disappear. A moment later the fin resurfaces and gleams within reach. Without thought he is his hands reaching. He grabs hold of the fin and with a roar pulls a young hammerhead shark six inches out of the water. The gills flare and the sickled tail cuts the ocean top as Bolivar roars at Hector for help, then roars at the youth again, but the shark slips from his grasp and falls in.

Bolivar stares as the ocean folds over the moment.

It is then he turns upon Hector.

He shouts, why didn't you help?

He moves towards Hector, his hands rising off his hips.

Hector does not look at him.

Bolivar roars. I said, what is wrong with you?

44

Hector turns and squeezes his hands so hard it looks as though he is wringing water from the finger-bones.

He says, I don't know, I just don't know.

Bolivar stares into the face before him.

Then he turns, paces up and down the boat feeling what just happened move inside him. The fin rising from nothing. The fin returning to nothing. How nothing gives to possibility. Something can come from nothing, he thinks. It is so.

He turns again upon Hector.

Look. This is what it is. It is not something else. It is not what you want it to be. It is what it is now and cannot be anything other. Do you understand?

Hector meets Bolivar's eye and nods.

If you do not understand then soon it will become something else again. You need to wake from the dream.

They watch marine debris pass beyond reach. Unidentified objects of different colours. What looks like a car tyre floating among tangled netting and line. Something inside Hector seems to waken. He stands with a light foot upon the trim as though ready to dive in but Bolivar pulls him back by the elbow.

He says, sharks are everywhere. You can't risk it.

When a plastic bag washes against the boat, Hector fishes it out. He finds within it a plastic engine fan, some copper wiring, an engine oil bottle that can be washed out. The same day he rescues with the plank a piece of styrofoam three feet long. He scrapes off the barnacles, pulls one out yellow and wriggling by the stalk.

Bolivar counts them.

He says, we will save half for tomorrow.

They chew carefully each mollusc.

Then Bolivar examines the wiring. Maybe we can use this as fishing gut if we strip the plastic. What do you think?

Hector reaches out. Let me have a look.

Bolivar takes the styrofoam and props his feet up on it and points to the ocean.

He says, this sea is like a supermarket.

The waters grow obscure. An ocean swell thickens and rolls the boat. What carries in the water is the dissipate energy of some distant storm. They watch the north-west horizon grow uncertain. Bolivar pointing to seabirds – a shearwater, then two fulmars that dive the wave-tops. He begins to smile. A sure sign of rain, he says.

All day Hector watches the sky and whispers. Slowly he gathers the cups and the engine oil bottle and arranges them on deck. He blesses himself. Sits pulling at his face, the tendons tight in the throat as he chews the inside of his cheeks.

When the waning moon ghosts the sky, Bolivar points towards it.

Look, he says. See how pale it is. The old wisdom says that is another sign.

They taste faraway rain. They watch lightning flare so remote it seems to belong to another age. By early morning, the hull is bone dry. Bolivar sits with his arms wrapped about his chest, a slow knotting in his temples.

Hector moves on hands and knees slowly about the hull, his tongue in search of dew. Then he sits and slumps forward pulling at his face.

When the sun opens the water, Bolivar grabs with bitten hands at triggerfish. He is silent now, the saliva gone, his mind growing absent. Then he lets out a small yip. He pulls into the boat a pale triggerfish. A bead of blood drips onto the hull and Hector's stare inhabits it, the eyes reading the moisture within the blood.

Bolivar cuts the fish into portions. They sit in the cooler and suck the juices out of the meat.

Afterwards, Bolivar stands and takes a plastic Coca-Cola bottle he has found in the water. He squeezes into it some drops of urine. Then he closes his eyes and puts it to his lips.

He says, so what if you drink your own piss. It will taste a little salty but it will get you by.

Hector's mouth opens and closes as though some thought has arrived but he has not the words to meet it.

Bolivar studies the youth's face. For sure, he thinks, the skull is growing longer. The eyes are losing their juice. I do not want to be rescued looking like this.

Hector sits looking at the sky.

He whispers, I am very cold.

A jet contrail thick as rope loosens and falls away.

At night Bolivar dreams his thirst. Dreams drinking water just beyond reach. Walking with an empty cup. The dryness spreading about the body – the flesh withering, the slowly baking bones, the blood turning to powder. He dreams he wakes in sudden panic before the absolute night sea. A fear in the dream that is the world moving beyond him. Then a voice speaks. It is a simple voice and sounds like his father. What the voice says.

You are a fisherman. It is a simple faith. The sea works its miracles.

Hector says, I have been having dreams where I am running all the time. Just running and running.

Bolivar turns and looks at Hector and sees he is asleep. He shakes the youth but Hector does not stir.

He slaps his own face.

Be careful, he thinks. You are losing your grip.

Bolivar rescues white plastic sheeting from the sea. It is crinkled and yellow with age. Hector folds it and climbs out of the cooler, puts it over his head. He sits sorting through sea junk. Bolivar leans out of the cooler and watches the youth twisting at wires. He can see Hector's shoulders are burnt. A footway of stones across water that is the spine leading to the skull.

Later, Hector stands up with a pleased look on his face. Bolivar stares and blinks upon a small figurine fashioned from wire and plastic. A blank face from the blade of a car fan. Strips of canvas for a headscarf. Wire looped into hands.

Bolivar says, what is it, some kind of voodoo?

He takes another sip of Coca-Cola, winces as the drink burns his lips. Then he begins to frown.

He says, you were supposed to strip that wire down.

Hector goes to speak but instead his eyes fall glazed upon the ocean. When he does speak it is not to Bolivar, it seems, but to the sea itself, his voice a whisper. His eyes upon the sea as though imploring it to listen.

My grandfather, Lito, he says. When I was a kid we used to visit him. He had a small place down south. There were times when the rain would not fall for weeks and weeks. He would make Mama carry the Virgin into the cornfield and he would pray that the rain would fall on his field but not on his neighbour's field across the road. Sometimes this would happen.

Bolivar stares at the figurine, the wires looped into supplicating hands. He stares at Hector's imploring face.

Hector says, we can ask the Virgin for help.

A gust of laughter escapes Bolivar's mouth. Then he shakes his head and puts it in his hands. When he looks up again he sees how Hector's eyes have narrowed, the mouth pulled into sneer.

Bolivar says, the sun has baked your brains.

Hector says, what would you know?

Bolivar meets the look in the youth's eye and holds it.

He says, you are right. I have known nothing all my life. I am only a fisherman. But I'll tell you this. It is ridiculous there is no rain. Out here it rains all the time. That is a fact. It is simply inevitable. A cloud will form any minute now. I can feel it.

Maybe a day. Bolivar boring at the sky with black eyes. Hector has fallen into a kind of stupor. A twitching in the pouted mouth. Then Hector leans forward and drops the Virgin idol out of his lap, falls without his hands out of the cooler. He lies there until Bolivar pulls him up, slaps him in the face.

He says, hey! Wake up. You can do this.

Later, he says, how much do you want to bet?

He shakes Hector.

I am willing to bet the first three sucks of a triggerfish it is going to rain tonight.

Hector sits closed off, his face a mask.

Upon the western waters, darkness spreading from light. Bolivar sits leaning forward. Then he pulls at Hector's arm.

He says, hey, wake up! You will not believe it. There is a change in the sky.

Hector opens his eyes but does not look up.

Bolivar squeezes Hector's arm.

He thinks, what comes to be comes in its own time and if you wish it nothing might happen.

Ears reach through sleep. Then Bolivar sits up. He climbs out of the cooler with his ear cocked, staring at the darkness.

Rain suddens upon the ocean and the waters roar. Bolivar wakes from nodding half-sleep, pulls Hector by the arm from the cooler. They fall upon the deck with the warm dawn rain falling into their mouths. The rain succulent upon the lips, the teeth, the tongue, the tongue licking the water off the lips, sucking on the teeth. Bolivar sees that Hector is crying and he thinks he might be crying also. It is hard to tell, he thinks, it might just be the rain on your face. A sob that is a rush of joy escapes his mouth.

He watches the youth kneel and give thanks with prayerful hands, the eyes squeezed shut, the mouth moving in silence. Then Hector pulls the idol to his chest.

Bolivar shouts, do you see now? We are really going to do this.

He begins to dance, grabs Hector by the shoulders, pulls him into a hug. A look of belief in the youth's face.

The sky gives all day. Pale and slicked, the men sit out and watch the cups fill. Bolivar following the feeling of the water swimming the blood, the blood swimming the heart and muscles, saliva loosening the tongue. They drink and watch the slow filling of the cups. They pour each filled cup into the five-gallon container and when the container is full, pour the water into the bailing bucket. The boat heaving upon a swell that sends a meniscus of water towards the bucket's brim. Hector trying to hold the bucket steady. Then Bolivar sits the bucket onto the plastic sheeting so that no water will be lost. He bundles the plastic around the lip. They stare at the bucket, at the ever-filling cups. Each bead of water that passes the lips, that fills the cups, that is filling the bucket, is a drop of time and life distilled.

During the night, the rain departs. The sound of the ocean resting again in an unhurried, ceaseless expression. Bolivar wakes and paces the deck. He stares at his sun-bronzed legs, his great hands, begins to think of himself as some sad, caged animal, something agleam still in the muscles. The eyes turning this way and that. The hands loose and empty.

He turns on Hector. Here, give me your cup. Let us start with this much water a day. I reckon there is enough to see us through until we are rescued. Some trawler or a giant container ship will come along. Wait till you see. It will rain soon again. For sure, our luck has turned.

In his sitting shape, Hector appears to be dozing or listening to his thoughts, but his face takes a sudden frowning look.

He says, it wasn't luck.

Huh? What are you talking about?

What you just said.

What?

That it was luck.

What was it then?

You saw what I did.

What?

You saw that I prayed.

Bolivar exhales and rolls his eyes.

He says, the sun has really cooked your skull. It was going to rain anyhow.

Hector stands up, folds his arms and turns away.

Schlik schlik. Schlik schlik. Bolivar wakes and the scratching sound stops. He peers into the half-light. There is Hector bent to the hull, the youth slowly leaning back on his haunches when he knows he is being watched. For a moment each self watches the other shadowed self as though each can see into the deep of the other, the private place of dream.

Then Hector climbs to his feet, steps into the sun as it sits upon the water at its lowest colour, his body robed in dawn light.

He says, good morning, captain.

He sits by the bow and sips a cup of water.

Bolivar continues to stare at Hector, an inscrutable smile on the youth's lips.

He sighs, then says, I didn't hear a single thing last night. I did not even dream.

As he speaks, a feeling rises within that tells him this is not true. Then he can see it, the dream again of his parents, this one worse than before – their house set alight and ravaged by fire, his parents alive but badly burnt. He stares into himself as though to meet the source of such horror but there is nothing to see within.

For a moment he meets a fear that what he saw in the dream was true.

He continues to stare at the youth with his hands on his hips. How Hector sits now with embered skin, the body slowly on fire. He can see how close Hector has come to death, the youth still a broken figure, his flesh coming out in sores. The light upon the body, the breathing body. The light falling as though beholding him in grace. It is then that Bolivar feels for Hector a rush of forgiveness. He is alive and not dead. I am alive too. We are still doing this. Maybe this is all a miracle, who knows.

He sits quietly, pretends not to see the new place on the boat where Hector has scored time.

Two weeks now, each week with a line through it. Another three days marked into the hull.

Just before dark, Hector rushes towards the trim with a shout. His eyes fixed upon a yellowed plastic bag afloat upon the indigo waters. Bolivar peers over his shoulder.

He says, we can reach it with the plank.

They find within the bag empty paint tins and a bamboo stirring stick, Japanese ideograms beneath slops of dried paint. Dead crabs fall out of the bag onto the deck.

Hector holds one up by the claw and sniffs.

Bolivar says, who knows how long those crabs are dead.

He takes the bamboo stick and begins to shave the tip into a spear. When it is done he hands it to Hector.

The youth stares at Bolivar with a long, gaunt look.

Slowly a smile appears.

The next day, Hector whoops and spears out a fish. It thrashes the deck in flecking yellowed green. Bolivar slaps his hands. I don't know what it is, he says. It looks like some type of mackerel. When Hector spears out another, Bolivar says, we can hang it up and let it air-dry.

Hector turns towards the Virgin idol. Within his eyes, a growing light.

Bolivar thinks, what is hope but a small flame. You feed it one small thing and then another. This is how we live.

He says, all I really know about you is that you are the son of Papi. You never really talk about yourself.

Hector shrugs. What is there to tell?

There must be something.

I don't know. What am I to say when you put me on the spot like this?

Tell me about your girlfriend. What does she look like?

I had a picture of her on my phone. The one you threw into the sea.

Bolivar opens his hands before him and shrugs as if to say, that was then and this is now. He stares at his open hands.

Look, he says. I am only trying to ask you.

The skin between Hector's brow begins to crease.

Then the youth speaks.

Listen, I don't know how to answer your questions. Each day now I am watching a part of me that is not a part of me. This is the part that is here. All the other parts of me are not here. They are back there. I do not know how to explain this. There is a part of me playing football right now. Another part of me is with Lucrezia. I am holding her hand as we watch some stupid thing she likes to watch on the TV. One of those soaps or whatever. A part of me is fighting with my parents. I am guessing it is about nine o'clock right now, so I am on the strip drinking beer. I am playing table football and speaking English with one of the gringo surfers. The part of me that is here is not here. It is back there. So I am not. But who I was back then is also not. Who I am not now is somebody else. But I don't know who he is. In some ways, he is still the son of Papi and Miriam and the brother of Rafael and Julia, but in other ways he is not. One is not the other. Do you see what I mean? I am not sure I fully understand this myself. No matter what way I look at it, I am not here and I am not there. I am not nothing but I am not anything either. So I am not-not. That is what I feel.

Bolivar blinks at Hector.

He tries to see into the words but the words thicken and grow obscure. He tries to see into the mind of the youth but can see only the skin on the bones that draw the face around the eyes in suffering.

He begins to knuckle his head.

Bolivar shouts and puts down the bamboo stick, reaches outside of the boat. What he pulls dripping out of the water is a green turtle as large as his chest. The turtle stares at them with a wizened expression, gestures some unfathomable thought with its flippers. Bolivar goes to work with the knife. He drains the blood into a cup, cuts open the flesh to find the stomach full of white plastic pellets. He cuts free the organs and portions the meat. He holds up the liver shining in his hand. Hector's face twists with disgust, he turns away and refuses to eat. Bolivar places the liver on the cowling and slices it into strips, puts a piece in his mouth and chews. He lets out a groan. It tastes so good, he says. He takes a sip of the blood and offers some but Hector shakes his head. He takes instead a sliver of raw leg meat and chews on it with a disgusted look. Then he stops and leans over and retches the food into his hand. When he lifts his face he is crying.

He says, I cannot eat this raw.

Bolivar takes the food and stares at Hector a long moment. Then he begins to smile. He takes the turtle shell and pretends it is a sunhat. Then an umbrella. Hector begins to grin, takes the shell and turns it into a kettle drum.

Then Bolivar pretends it is a large telephone.

Hello? Yes. I am hoping you can patch me through. I want to put in an order for a crate of beer and a rescue boat. Yes, within the hour. Thank you.

It is the hour of the world's vanishing. Bolivar watches until there is nothing to see. Then he closes his eyes. He can see himself standing in Gabriela's bar. Telling Rosa and Angel. The others leaning in. He can feel a joint hanging from his lips. A wash of smoke in his lungs. He sees himself moving his hands as he tries to explain. He sees himself pointing towards the beach. *What you do has no effect upon it. I've always known, but yet— And still you are a part of it. The fish as to the sea, the sea as to the fish.* He grasps a cold glass of beer, rinses his mouth with the malt taste, licks his teeth. He spreads his hand upon Rosa's lower back and she moves closer to him. *The ocean is. You are also. But the ocean always is, it is never not.* He opens his eyes. He can sense Hector puzzling at him in the dark. The drooping face. *What is given shape by the body is the telling of the man.* This is what he tells Angel and Rosa. *The story of the man is told by the body. Look at Hector and you know what he is.* He studies the imprint of the youth's body as he sits in the dark. He tries to sense the spirit under the skin. He thinks about Hector catching the fish. He thinks about the spirit rising within him. What is alive now and growing within the youth. *For sure he is not like you, Angel, but he is not a bad skin. He is not some insect pest. He is my friend.*

A distant light on dark sea. Passing by, unreachable, a ship.

Days of hammering sun, the sea the sun's anvil. Hector sits in the cooler chewing air-dried turtle meat. He loosens his mouth with water. When he speaks it is barely over the breath.

Just eight days till Christmas.

Bolivar begins to shake his head.

He says, I cannot believe it.

Then he says, look, we will be rescued by then. I know it. Some kind of vessel. Like the one that passed by the other night.

I just don't know. How can you know? There is no knowing any more.

Hector climbs out of the cooler and kneels before the Virgin idol. Bolivar visors a hand against the sea's sparkling light and studies the youth. The burnt shoulder skin has bronzed. A sore weeps like an eye.

He climbs out and sprinkles seawater onto the last of the turtle liver.

Then Hector turns and watches Bolivar.

He says, I would love a swim.

Me too.

We could try it. I am a very good swimmer. Just stay by the boat.

No. You will bring the sharks up.

Damn it. I am going in.

Hector grabs hold of the trim with a decided look.

Bolivar moves quickly, takes him by the elbow but speaks quietly.

Don't do it, brother.

Bolivar tries to hold the youth with a warning look, the sea whispering, something within the youth changing before him, a hardening in the eyes that Bolivar can see. Then Hector begins to nod.

He lifts his hands off the trim.

OK, he says. OK.

Bolivar smiles.

He says, look, we will celebrate Christmas here. It will be the greatest of all celebrations. We will skip the midnight feast and eat in daylight instead. It will be memorable. You will speak of it for years to come. You will see.

A gauze of rain slowly fills the cups. In sleep Hector hears something strike the boat. He climbs out of the cooler blinking against the rain-dark. Steps into moonlight spread thinly on the panga. It is then he can see it, a shadowed thing, something rounded, passing by the hull. He grabs hold of it, shouts for Bolivar to wake.

They haul it in dripping and dark. Bolivar cursing, for something has sliced open his finger. He puts his finger to his mouth and enjoys the taste of blood.

I hope it's some type of hook, he says.

They must wait till dawn to see what it is.

The unfolding light reveals a great tangle of debris – old nets and fishing line, faded plastic bottles and bags, hundreds of stinking dead crabs. Hector reaches into the debris and pulls free a tangled pair of tights, then the bleached and headless body of a doll. Bolivar begins to pull at the flotsam. How in places it seems as though the sea with infinite patience has grafted one thing onto another, the sea slowly working until all things become single matter.

Hector smiles brightly. He says to Bolivar, this is a gift from God.

A day is spent cutting and untangling webs of netting. Bolivar fumbling with thick fingers. He snorts and climbs to his feet. You are better at doing this, he says. Hector does not look up. He sits at a slight lean with an unblinking gaze. Bolivar begins to pace the deck. Then with the knife he cuts at snarls of fishing line. He knots them into a new line and wraps the line around some wood. Then he ties to the line a metal sinker and a hook fashioned from the engine spring.

Hector works without word, his fingers moving like a crab, the sun dialling around his body until he spreads out a makeshift net. It stretches half the length of the boat and is hued it seems of every colour. Bolivar runs it through his hands. Here and there he pulls the knotting tighter.

Hector says, it isn't so bad.

Bolivar says, it will do.

He ties the net to the bitt. Then he takes a piece of metal from the motor and clove-hitches it as weight to the net. Again he tests the net's strength. They stare at it for a moment before they let it run. All night they can hardly sleep, each man taking turns to climb out in the dark and test the net. And when they do sleep it is of the net that each man dreams.

In the half-light Bolivar begins to shout. A silvered skip-jack tuna has been caught. Hector stoops out of the cooler and pulls back his hair to reveal a grin. He begins to whoop and jump, rocking the boat until Bolivar puts his hand up. Take it easy, he says. He untangles the fish and watches it slap about the deck. Hector bends and prods at the glazed skin, pokes at a fin, runs his finger down the fatty loin.

When Bolivar slides the knife into the flesh, the incision jets a spurt of blood. He puts his hand into the fish, pulls out the heart and places it on the deck. He drains the blood into a cup but the heart of the fish continues to beat in reflex. Slowly Bolivar works the knife through the flesh but the heart still beating free of the body calls out to them. They stare at it, this heart that can never go back into the body and yet still it beats.

Look at that, Bolivar says. Even in death the heart doesn't give up.

Bolivar stares at the sea and gives thanks. The sea is a giving thing, the net is doing its work. One tuna and then another, other types of fish that could be this or that. One time, a glossy young tiger shark. A handful of fish that glitter as though made of sand. Hector lays one in the palm of his hand and runs the flesh with his finger.

Bolivar fills the pair of tights with fish cuttings and hangs the meat to air-dry. Under the sun they slow-bake fish laid out on the cowling. Then Bolivar winds in the line to find the fashioned hook has gone. He stares at the sea a moment then shrugs. It is not so bad, he says. We have more fish than we can eat. Seabirds have begun to circle the boat. Now and then a bird lands on the trim and Bolivar shoos it away.

He sits savouring the moisture of the tuna. Then he takes a sup of water and swirls it in his mouth. He watches Hector as he eats, the long fingers putting the food into the mouth. The mouth closed in chewing. Something alight now in the eyes. A growing fire.

Bolivar says, maybe we should give her a name.

Who?

The lady.

Hector stares at the stocking full of fish.

Bolivar runs his hand down the lady's leg.

I think I am in love, he says.

He slaps his thigh and leans back and laughs.

Then he leans forward with a sudden serious look.

He says, it is strange to say it, but this is good, is it not? What I mean is, it is very simple. Nothing else. We are making it work out until we are rescued.

Hector finishes chewing then slowly swallows. He says, it is amazing what you can get used to. We have enough

food and drink to last a couple of weeks. We have shelter.
Every so often it rains. The sea is generous. I really think
we can do this. I really think we can hold on until we are
rescued by a ship.

Bolivar nods.

Yes, he says. We will be rescued. That is a fact.

During the night, when Hector is asleep, he climbs out
of the cooler and gently touches the lady's leg but feels no
response in his body.

Bolivar watches the wilderness of sea, the world vast to its
seam. The eyes hoping always for a passing boat, a trawler
or a ship.

He thinks, what is life but waiting.

He closes his eyes and listens.

Always waiting upon the awaited thing. But what if
you hold what is given?

Watching how the wave travels then folds, falls upon
another that carries the passing energy within it, the life
and death of the sea.

Now and then a silent delight rushes through him.
A feeling that begins to speak. That life on the panga
isn't so bad. That out here, for the first time, everything
has fallen away. The weight you carry in your heart.
The longing in the body for a woman. The pain and
problems of living. He begins to imagine all those lost at
sea. Those whom he knew or had heard of. Slim Martin
and Francisco the Cat. Luis Fernando and Manuel the
Harelip and Old Frank. Their fathers and their fathers

before them. Perhaps they were not lost at all but lived on like this, adrift for years, adrift into old age, drifting farther and farther out to sea yet keeping themselves alive, a simple life lived on rainwater and fish. Perhaps this is so. Perhaps they are alive still.

I cannot believe it is Christmas, Hector says. He shakes his head in disbelief, then puts the Virgin idol on the seat, closes his eyes and begins to pray. When he opens his eyes he rests them vacantly upon the sea. Again he shakes his head. He speaks but his voice sounds far away.

All the things they were doing at home last night.

Bolivar turns and studies the horizon. He sees how the day has unfolded simply, the sun climbing into position, the ocean as it is. He thinks, today might be Christmas Day but also it might not.

He turns and studies Hector, sees within the eyes the youth walking among the ghosts of his people.

Bolivar leaps up and slaps his hands together. A grin wrinkles his eyes.

Look, he says. Today will be the greatest Christmas ever. We will prepare a feast. There will be all the usual things and some special things also. You will see. You know the story about the three shepherds? Wait till you hear my version. It is the funniest thing ever.

Then Bolivar produces something from under the

stern seat. He says, I made this for you. Hector stares at a face scratched into driftwood. The eyes crinkled in laughter. The mouth a wide grin.

Hector stands looking at the wooden face and then he holds it to his chest.

It is perfect, he says.

Then his face falls and takes on a sorrowful look.

I did not make you anything.

Bolivar pours double rations of water. He presents fresh barnacles, then strips of sun-dried tuna and strips of a young mahi-mahi caught two days before. He waves his hand over some shark meat that is beginning to smell. Pinch your nose, he says, and you can pretend it is something else. Bolivar rubs his hands then eats with abandon, his eyes closed, his tongue slapping about his mouth. Hector slowly chews the food. He eats with his eyes squeezed as though concentrating all his attention upon it.

They sing some songs they both know and Bolivar tells some stories, this thing that happened to me one time, you will not believe it.

Later, Hector points at Bolivar's arm. That faded tattoo, he says. Is it a woman's name?

Bolivar studies for a moment the bleached green tattoo on his forearm as though he has not noticed it for a long time. He runs an index finger along the skin then shrugs.

He says, it is the name of a woman, that is all.

Hector says, who is she? What happened to her?

Bolivar leans forward and laughs.

Nothing happened to her. She is the mother of my daughter. Maybe that is what happened to her.

You have a child?

It is then that Bolivar stops smiling.

He says, I do. Or maybe I did. I don't know any more which one it is. I did have a daughter. Maybe I still do. Either way, she does not know me. I guess that means I no longer have a child. Maybe it is the case that I have a daughter but she doesn't have a father. Yes, that is probably it.

Bolivar reads from Hector's expression a question arising from the risen brows, the way he leans slightly forward with an open mouth.

Bolivar puts up the flat of his hand.

Look, man. I don't like where this conversation is going. It gives me a pain in the head.

That was the best day yet, Hector says. He is making himself comfortable within the cooler, trying to stretch an arm out, wriggle a shoulder. Bolivar blankets seaweed up to his neck. Then Hector goes to speak but stops, Bolivar sensing still within the youth the unspoken question. You should have said nothing, he thinks. It is none of his business. Do not tell him a thing.

Then Hector says, Lucrezia — I wonder what she is doing. If she is thinking about me. Maybe she is, maybe she is not. Probably now she is with him.

With who?

This other guy. I keep thinking she is with him while I am stuck here. I cannot stop these thoughts. All the time

67

I have them. She is hard work, let me tell you. Truthfully, I do not know if I even like her all that much. I like it when I am with her but then I forget about her when she is not around. Tell me, why is that? Why am I like this? Tell me, is it normal for a girl not to want to fool around? Sometimes I think I will go crazy. She never lets me into her bedroom. We sit and watch TV and whenever I try and do something she slaps my hands away. She never lets me do a single thing. She says she is not ready. She says it is a sin. She says she is having her period. She says all sorts of things. Sometimes I really think I am going to go crazy. I dream about it all the time. What it would be like even though my body now is not interested. She keeps telling me, wait, you must wait, Hector. But wait for what? I would like to know. Sometimes I think she is lying. There is this guy, Octavio. He is four years older than me. I see him around. He is a welder or something. I saw him leaving her house one time when her parents were out. I ask her, what was he doing here? And she says, he was dropping something off for my brother. But this guy and her brother hardly know each other. It does not make sense. Another time I see them in the car together. Octavio's car. I do nothing for days but I imagine his hands all over her. She is letting him do these things. I say to her, I am done with you, I know what you are. But she pulls a shocked face, says to me, he was only giving me a lift to my nan's. It is not my fault you have a sick mind. Maybe we should not see each other any more. Then I go crazy and want to see her even more. She has an answer for everything.

Bolivar is silent a moment. Then he says, I don't know, Hector. Maybe you need to be careful. If you ask me, the river sounds because it is carrying water. Do you know what I mean? Women are tricky, but so are men. If you ask me, we are as useless as each other.

Hector says, I would love to tell her, you made us wait too long and now it is too late. This is what you have done. At least I could have taken that with me. I could have known what it was like.

They lie in the cooler shiftless and awake. Then Bolivar sighs and begins to speak.

Look, I did not always live on the strip. I had another life before this one. And yes, I had a little girl. But that is all there is to it.

He stops speaking, sits within an inward gaze that travels to where he used to live.

He opens his eyes and stares at the moon trembling upon the water.

He tries not to think.

He thinks, do not tell him anything.

He says, look. I come from some other place. But I do not want to talk about it. I used to think about this place where I come from all the time but then I began to forget. It is easier like this. You can teach yourself to do it. Every man has the right to change his life. It is not unusual. Sometimes it is for the best. Yes. I was married once. Maybe I still am. Maybe I am not. Who knows. Maybe that little bishop who looked like he'd been struck by lightning dissolved the marriage. Or maybe she thinks I am dead and she married someone else, she is now a big-amist, who is to know. For sure she will think I am dead if ever she hears about this. It hurts me to think about it. Yes, I have a daughter. I left her. No, that is not it. I had to go away. Yes. I had to leave her. It was a choice I had to make, one thing or another. Anyhow, she is called Alexa. I named her myself. I named her because when I first saw her, she looked like an Alexa. It is hard to explain this feeling. You cannot know it until you hold your own child.

He reaches out his hand in the dark.

She was this high when I left her.

Where is she now? Why did you leave?

Do not ask me so many questions. I am tired. It is the middle of the night. It has been a long day. The best Christmas ever. Look, I do not know all the answers. You do some things in your life. That is all I know.

Bolivar is almost asleep when Hector's voice reaches in the dark.

She is with him. She is with him for sure.

Bolivar clears his voice and says, how can you be sure?

She will be delighted I am gone.

Look. You cannot know anything. What can you know out here? Nothing. It is impossible. Let me tell you, it will be a big deal to many, many people that you were washed out to sea. For me, not so many people will care. But for you, let me tell you, your people will be praying for weeks and weeks. It will never end. There will be novenas and endless visits and she will be among them praying. She will be kneeling before her bed with her hands clasped pleading with God every night. She will be wishing she had done all those things with you. She will be asking God's permission to do all those things if you return. And if she has done you any wrong, she will be drowning in guilt. She will blame herself. She will think you are innocent. She will dump that guy in an instant. That is how these things go. I have seen it myself many times.

He will be able to do what he likes with her now.

You need to stop this. You will drive yourself crazy. Here, eat some of this fish.

Hector is silent, then sighs.

Maybe you are right, Bolivar. You are such a good friend.

They watch the sun slide into the sea, a container ship ghosting within it.

Bolivar does not notice and then he does. He has stopped telling time by the sun. His mind falling into slowness. Time now is not time. It does not pass but rests. This is what he thinks. The days now passing within an arresting of time. Or sometimes he thinks time is passing without him, passing overhead or around him or underneath but not within. He tries to reason it out, how it is like some enormous thing, something unaccountable to all thought, action or utterance. You have been cut off from its passing and yet it continues and always will. He studies Hector to see if this could be true for him also.

Then come days when he meets a soaring happiness. A feeling from within of possibility and freedom. It is summoned by each burning dawn, the world from ashes coming to be again. They watch the earth remake itself in splendours of colour and grow quiet in astonishment. How it seems such skies have never been witnessed. A stillness growing between Bolivar and Hector that is also an understanding. Each man beginning to see the truth of the other, that each is as helpless within the truth of all this. That what a man carries in his heart has no consequence within such vastness. And yet the heart bloods the wish. Hector always watching the sea. Each glittering of light a possible sighting. But more and more often now Bolivar rests his eyes. He speaks to himself the feeling that it could always be like this. What need is there of much else? You eat and you sleep and you do simple tasks. Now we are truly alive.

Hector says, I dreamed last night I was home in my bed. In the dream it was morning and it was time to get up. But when I left my room I saw that the house was empty. It had been empty for a long time – my parents gone, my brother and sister gone, a layer of dust upon everything. In the dream they had been dead for many years and it happened while I was gone. I walked through the empty house. Then I woke. What do you think this dream means? I am afraid that something is wrong back home.

Bolivar says, I keep having a dream where I am burying

dead bodies. I am in the hills behind the town where I used to live before I went to the coast. In the dream I am measuring the size of a grave. I do this by lying on the ground and marking out around my body with a stick. I think I understand the meaning of this dream. But when I wake and look at the sea I can see that my own size is nothing within it, that no size can be marked upon the ocean nor recognised.

Hector says, that sounds to me like a stupid dream.

Bolivar's sleeping body senses the changing weather. He wakes alone in the cooler. *Schlik schlik. Schlik schlik.* He leans out to see Hector a shadowed thing bent to the hull. Bolivar studies the youth a moment, then climbs out muttering under his breath. He watches the gloom that hangs over the world. The sea become lead.

He takes from under the stern seat the plastic bags harvested from the sea. He smooths them out and cuts them carefully with the knife into strips. Then he braids the strips into rope. He frees some fish gut from the ball of debris and knots the gut and the braided rope together, cuts a hole in the sheeting and runs the rope beyond it. Then he secures this rope around the cooler and knots it.

Hey, he shouts. Look at this.

Hector looks up and sees Bolivar flapping a doorway.

*

They shudder through some endless squall. Days like nights of ancient rain. Bolivar trying to keep hold of the doorway as the downpour rushes in. They are damp through and huddle under a seaweed blanket, their teeth clacking, their skin grey and wrinkled. Hector with the Virgin idol in his lap. He grows quiet, has been shiftless and awake most of the night. Each time he moves he nudges Bolivar in the ribs. He switches his legs, recrosses his arms, wraps them about his chest. A wheeze now sits at the edge of his breath. Then he grows motionless, spends a day staring bird-eyed at the sheet as though trying to see through it. He begins to whisper something unintelligible. He whispers it over and over until Bolivar shouts at him to stop.

Then Hector speaks it aloud.

I know what she is doing.

Bolivar leans closer. Who?

Lucrezia. She is with him.

With who?

Octavio.

Bolivar lets out a long sigh. Then he squeezes his hands.

Look, he says. You need to stop this. It is impossible to know what she is doing. We are as good as blind out here.

No. It is simple to work out.

How?

Today is a Saturday.

How is it a Saturday? Out here, there are no days of the week.

I have been keeping track of the days. Today is a Saturday, for sure. Do not ask me how I know this. It is the afternoon. This is the time she would be with me. We would be watching a game show or something stupid on TV. One of her soaps. But now I am here and he is there.

But how can you know?

It is easy, Bolivar. Her parents do the shopping at this time. She has nothing else to do. So she watches TV. But she has this weird thing – she cannot watch TV on her own. She likes to do it with somebody else. So she will invite him over. He will park his car farther down the street. It is simple to work out. He will come into the house and he will watch TV with her. But he will not do this for long. He will sit and pick at the frills on the arm rest. He will pick at the dog hairs and let them fall onto the carpet. Then he will say to her, let's go to your room. And she will say, let me watch the end of this. He will wait, then he will say again, it is over now, let's go. She will take a look at the front door and be silent a moment listening for their car. He will say, they are not due back for some time. She will look at Octavio's face, look at his hands, and she will think what it would be like to have those hands all over her. That is when she will take him to her room. They are there now.

Bolivar is studying Hector as he speaks. Even in this dim light he can see how the eyes dream outward in agony. How the eyes seem to project onto the sheet what the mind sees inward.

What the mind believes.

He shakes the youth's arm.

It cannot be true, he says. There is no way of knowing.

Hector pushes Bolivar back with the flat of his hand.

Do not tell me what is true or not.

Here, eat some food.

I am not hungry.

Bolivar begins to shake his head. Then he climbs out to check the rain cups. They are near full. He pours the water into the container then stands a moment squeezing his fists. When he returns he is still vexed.

Look, he says. They are still thinking about you back home. Every day now they are praying for your return. I can assure you, she is too. You need to think about this. You need to think healthy thoughts. You are not looking so well. Listen to your breath. You need nourishment. Here. Eat a piece of this.

Hector does not answer but continues to stare at the sheet.

After some time, he speaks in a remote voice.

She is doing things to him.

Bolivar climbs outside and checks the cups, feels the warm air on his skin. The world in earliest light. It is often like this, a molten slow-pouring of colour. A feeling of time as though the world were coming into being. He stretches his arms and legs and listens to the sea, comes to believe he can hear something whispered from long ago. He is thinking all the time of Alexa. How she moves inside him as a shadowed being. Who she might be now in the world. He turns and quietly studies Hector curled in the cooler like a child. A hand resting against the mouth. He bends to study the face. His eyes travelling the forked brow, the eyelids flickering at some dream.

An older voice within him asks, what is the meaning of Hector?

Day after day he is meeting such thoughts that are strange to him. It is always an older voice that speaks.

He thinks, he is somebody's child.

For days, he watches the youth, not the spindled arms and legs, not his sulky demeanour. But something within the youth he is trying to see. An essence, perhaps. A sign of the life force within. The living will, he thinks, that meets the living will of others. He can see Hector moving among his people. His words spoken, the simple gestures. A nod of the head, a smile, a wince, a shrug of indifference. A going forward to do this thing or that, or a not-doing, a refusing, a sitting among them, just being in the same room. The will in meeting with the will of others, each action or non-action a bond with his people.

This is the source of his meaning, he thinks. The life force that is the will unwatched, unnoticed, unquestioned. The will in the world.

But his will is out here.

The will has seen itself.

He is not sure if he understands this or what it might mean.

Then he shakes his head.

Why can he not have meaning out here?

Bolivar begins to see his own life. How he was once a part of this living will among others.

He thinks of how he removed himself from his family, his daughter, all the people he knew, put an absence in the place of his being.

He thinks, you took yourself away from your meaning.

Alexa's eyes. He can see them watching the space where he used to be.

For the first time he begins to feel grief for his child.

He can feel the grief she will carry inside her all her life. His mother and his father watching the space he once inhabited.

He closes his eyes and thinks, what is it I have done? Maybe it is not too late to do something.

A single word resounding in his mind.

Papa.

Something within him wakens. He begins to watch the sea with fevered eyes. As he sits he holds a vision of himself, can see himself leaving the strip to return home, prodigal and repentant.

He weeps quietly into his fist.

Hector watching, unsure what to do. He puts a hand to the other man's shoulder in comfort.

He says, it is OK, Bolivar. Here, eat this. You are not so fat as you used to be.

At night Bolivar listens to Hector weeping also.
Grief is a thing that sits shapeless between them.
Bolivar says, pain is a dog that follows you no matter
where you go.
He shakes himself, wipes his eyes with his wrist.
We are like a pair of old women, he says. We need to
stop this blubbering. It uses up moisture.

Bolivar stands up and walks about and sits down again. He
feels the need to speak. He holds Hector's eye and does
not blink.
He says, I dream about my daughter now every night.
Who she might be. I dream about the emptiness I left
behind. I guess now she is fourteen years old.
He falls silent.
Then he says, I do not think I can talk about it.

Later, he says, look, it is very common. You have a child
with a woman and the relationship doesn't work. There
is a problem. The woman wants to have the man with
her mind but the love has gone from her body. The man
finds himself shut out. There are many men this happens
to. No, that is not it. Look, I left because of who she was,
that woman. She changed. She became interested only in
the child. I ceased to exist. What was left of me she tried
to control by ignoring me. I could not live any more.
Anyhow, she snored in her sleep. Her snoring was so loud
it used to rattle my skull. I could not take it any more.
I began to lose sleep. Then I began to sleep in another

room. Then I began to sleep elsewhere. There was this
widow. She was young enough. There was room in her
bed. Then one day I was gone. It was that simple. Please
don't look at me like that. Don't expect me to know why
I do these things. I am only a fisherman.

Later, he says, look, there was nothing to do, no work
to be found. It made sense to do a little work for them,
that is all. The cartel. To see what it would be like. They
have money, you know. Cars, women, the easy life, all the
good things. You look at the system and see how it is
rigged against you. The system does not want you to live.
A friend of mine got involved. One day he was a *no* man
and the next day he was a *yes* man. He began to lead the
good life. Then he asked me to do a few things. Small
things. Just do this thing for me, Bolivar, he says. It is not
a big deal. Keeping watch on this place or that. Driving
somebody in a jeep. Visiting the premises of some place
or other. Giving some guy a good beating – somebody
who didn't pay up – this is what happens. You get used
to it. Then I began to go out with them at night. I saw
things. We were up in the hills. This one thing, I saw, one
night. What they told me to do. That was when a bad
feeling began to come over me. I could feel it like some
slow poison entering my blood. It began to eat into my
bones. I could not sleep any more. I could not look myself
in the eye. How can you be *you* when you are with *them*?
You are no longer *you*. You have become *them*. So how
can you say *no*? You have said *yes* to them. If you say *yes*
it means *yes*. If you say *no* it means *yes*. If you say *maybe*

it means *yes*. If you keep your mouth shut it means *yes*.
If you are dead it is because they said *yes* for you. Before
you stands only this one word *yes*. And yet I knew within
my heart that I had to say *no* even though this word *no*
did not exist. I went away where nobody could find me.
I went on foot. Many days and nights. I said it to myself
over and over, *I am a no, not a yes!* I said it with every step
until I arrived at the coast with nothing but the clothes on
my back. Maybe a little money as well. But look. I could
make a simple living on the strip. A man and a boat, yes, it
is simple living, this is good, no complications, nothing to
haunt your dreams or keep you awake at night. Each day
is a simple matter. You are presented with a choice. Do I
fish or not? This type of life suited me. That is why I left.

Hector leans forward in the dark and asks in a low
voice. What happened up in the hills?

Bolivar is silent. Then he speaks.

Do not ever ask me that.

Hector does not sleep. Or if he sleeps he is met with
visions that shake his whole body so that he moves as
though awake. He mutters and coughs and twists. Then
in quarter-light, Hector suddenly climbs out of the cooler
and walks about the boat. He returns and grabs Bolivar's
arm, fixes him with a piercing look.

He says, I think I am losing my mind. Again and again
I keep having the same dream. I dream I am in the boat.
And then I wake and find I am *still* in the boat. When this
happens I cannot breathe. I go out and walk around the
boat until I can breathe again. Then there are times when

I have the same dream but I cannot wake up. In the dream there is this great panic to wake. I know in the dream that when I wake everything will be all right. Sometimes I am able to think of something to wake me up. But then when I wake, I see I am still in the boat and that I am waking into another dream that is the same as before. This is when I really panic. Then I wake but I do not know what is real any more. I think I have seen movies like this. There is no escape.

Later, Hector says, tell me, Bolivar, why would God be so cruel? Make you dream like this? Keep you neither alive nor dead? Tell me, why would God do this?

I do not know, Hector. How can I know? I do not know the answer to these things. You need to ask a priest or something. Where can we find a priest?

Bolivar seems to laugh a little.

He climbs out and checks the rain cups. The five-gallon container and bucket are full. He takes a drink from a cup and brings it to Hector.

Here drink this.

Hector takes the cup in silence.

Then he says, tell me, Bolivar, who is the dreamer?

He turns and stares at Bolivar but does not appear to see him. His skin is a yellow-grey colour.

Bolivar begins screwing his eye sockets with his fists. Then he pulls and twists the wires of his beard.

He says, what sort of question is that?

Hector says, I am watching my life but I cannot live it. So I have decided this must be a dream. It is the only thing that makes sense to me. But what I cannot figure out is this – am I dreaming or is God dreaming it? Or maybe it is the Devil. In which case, it makes no difference. But if I am dreaming then surely I can wake. The question is, how can I do this? If God is dreaming this then I cannot wake. It is up to him.

Bolivar stops breathing as he listens to Hector. His face darkens. The eyes tighten with a look of puzzled apprehension.

I do not understand you. How is this a dream? I am here. Look—

He leans forward and pinches Hector's forearm.

The youth pulls his arm away.

See. You are awake.

Hector nods without expression.

He says, yes, but that does not prove anything.

Later, Hector says, maybe I am not ready to wake.

That is why she is with him. I have to suffer until he decides to wake me. I think I see this now. This is my purgation.

He climbs out of the cooler, an edge of wind lifting the hair from his face. Then he turns towards Bolivar who has followed him out of the cooler and is looking at him now with sad, alert eyes. Hector begins to nod.

He says, if this is my dream, I can do what I like. If this is God's dream, I can also do what I like because he will not allow me to wake until he decides.

Hector stands in the rain watching the world with an unreadable expression.

He says, I will show her. I will make sure she never forgets me.

It is then he lets out a strange and rich laugh.

Bolivar feels a tremble run through his body.

What is in the laugh, he thinks. What is in the eyes of the laugher.

The sea is loosening their net. For days there is no catch. Bolivar hauls in the net and Hector combs through it, retying the knots. Bolivar keeping watch of a fulmar circling overhead. Again and again he has found the bird upon their air-drying fish. He keeps shooing at it, the bird watching him with black eyes as though it cannot see. He thinks about what he is or isn't in the sight of the bird. He stares into Hector's eyes. This feeling now that something has changed within the youth. He wonders about what is or isn't in Hector's mind. He stares at the eyes and what he sees is the creeping yellow that has begun to infect the whites of Hector's eyes.

Bolivar meets in sleep the need to run. He dreams that his legs can't move. When he wakes he is met with the inescapable weight of the body. All this time sitting about, he thinks. You are like an old man. Is this how you want to look when you return? You must get fit. You must strengthen the muscles. Then you will be fit for anything.

Hector twists and mutters in his sleep.

Bolivar begins to move with heavy steps. Fire in the far sky. Fire in the weight of the legs. Slowly he laps the cooler. Fire reaching into the heart and lungs. As dawn begins to brighten the boat, he arrives slowly at the strip. He runs through the trees and breathes the light. The dawn light upon the breathing green.

He thinks, we will go to Gabriela's for a drink, see who is about.

His breathing finds a saw-tooth rhythm. He is able to run with half-closed eyes. The lagoon safe behind the trees. The path solid to his feet. He is running towards the bar but soon he is short of breath and he stops and clings to the gunwale. He opens his eyes. It is then he sees where Hector has scratched time into the hull by the under-edge of the seat. The marks are neat and hard to see. He frowns and leans closer, begins to count.

He hears himself mutter. It cannot be so.

He begins to pull at his hair.

He counts again and then looks for the knife, begins to scratch out the lines.

He sits and repeats the time in his mind.

He looks up and asks, how can this be so?

Seventy-three days.

Bolivar sits gutting a tuna pulled from a rippling sea, the first fish in days. Hector leaning a wolfish look over the trim. Then he begins to yell. Bolivar follows the pointed finger with a squinted eye. What he sees is a yellow plastic barrel. It is then that Hector climbs upon the gunwale and without word dives into the water. Bolivar gasps, reaches out his hands, watches with a lurching nausea as the youth begins to swim. He tries to shout but the air won't release. He leans forward and grips the gunwale with both hands.

Time rushing into slowness. Bolivar watching every inch of the water as Hector swims with hooking, unhurried arms. Finally the youth seizes hold of the barrel and rolls his body over it, laughing and shouting. Bolivar finds his voice, roars out, keep your eyes open!

Hector begins to swim with the barrel.

It is slow work, pushing the barrel, kicking his long legs.

Then he grows tired, stops and rests against the container. Bolivar watching as Hector turns and lies on his back treading water. The youth staring at the sky with his long limbs spread as though suddenly transported, he is back at the strip, he is lounging in the shallows at the beach. Bolivar pulls at his hair. He climbs upon the stern seat and roars at Hector to hurry. It is then the youth stirs and begins to swim, the long limbs tired now, the body heavy.

Bolivar pulls the barrel with both hands into the boat. He lets Hector haul himself in. The youth stands in the sun, wheezing and spent yet immense with himself. A coating of light upon the wet body. He stares at Bolivar with his yellowed eyes utterly alive. Then he throws his head back and laughs. It is that same strange, rich laugh.

Bolivar cannot speak, turns his back on Hector.

He begins to examine the barrel, lifts the lid and takes a deep inhale.

It smells like some kind of cooking oil, he says. I reckon you can put fifty gallons in there.

Hector moves to the barrel and peers in.

It is then that Bolivar grabs the youth by the wrist and meets him eye to eye.

Bolivar says, do not do that to me again.

Hector meets the look with yellowed eyes that light out of the thinning body, the wet hair sculpted to the bones of the face. He shakes Bolivar off and turns and spreads himself out on the seat to dry, one knee risen upon the seat, the left hand draping down in falling with his hair.

The whites of Hector's eyes deepen fully into yellow. He has grown fearless in the water. He slides into the dusk waters to cool and does not listen to Bolivar's pleading. What you are doing isn't right. You are going to get killed. What will I do on my own?

Later, Bolivar looks up and calmly points to a vortex of roiling small fish.

The sea cut by fin.

He watches how the youth does not turn to look but sits with the yellowed eyes of a wolf, hunting upon some thought with a faraway look.

A disturbed smell on the wind. Bolivar studies the waters and the sky, watches a greyness gather in the east. They haul in the net and find a third of it gone. Bolivar closes his eyes and counts. Just one fish in six days. They repair the net as best they can and let it out.

When they are finished, Hector slides into the sea, a blithe shadow parting the evening waters.

Bolivar watching, squeezing his hands into fists, watching until he cannot see Hector. He stands upon the bow seat and stares at the molten light as it cools upon the water, his eyes taken to the farthest reaches, but Hector cannot be seen and there is nothing to witness. For an instant he is met with a feeling that Hector never was and that he has dreamed all this. He pulls at his hair and closes his eyes and then he begins to roar. He waves with great sweeping arms, steps towards the edge ready to dive in but his legs will not move. He looks at his legs and beats his thighs, then climbs back down and sits in a defeated slump.

It cannot be true, he says. It cannot happen like this.

He punches the sides of his legs.

You are a coward. He is not a coward.

Maybe. He is not a coward but he is a fool.

Yes. You are not a fool.

Just then the waters stir behind him. He turns to see Hector climbing sunken-chested over the dark side of the boat. The knife and some barnacles in his hand. The youth coming to be with a serene and glassy look. His yellowed skin intensified by the evening light. With two hands he sluices the water off his body.

He says, that swim has done me good.

Bolivar seizes Hector with a murderous look but the youth calmly turns away.

*

A dark crosshatched sea. Bolivar watches the sky with a grim look as the panga lurches upon a swell. He scratches at his neck until he breaks the skin. Then he turns and unties the Jolly Roger from the trim, throws it to Hector. Put your sweater on, he says. He unties the last of their stockinged fish and puts it in the cooler. He gathers the cups and their belongings and puts them in plastic bags and ties them to the hooks under the seat. He screws tight the lid upon the yellow water barrel. Then he pulls in the net and ties it around the bitt. Hector kneeling before the Virgin idol. They sit and watch the dark gather the far sky, the dark advancing.

The known shape of the world, their voices, the boat. All unbecome in the flung dark-sound of the sea. They lie in the cooler clutched together. The wind funnelled into a wail. Down the troughs of sea. Down the blind and bottomless fear that rests in the heart of each man. The panga then heaving upward. Hector refusing to bail. Bolivar furious, climbing out to check the rain barrel. He stands for a moment willing himself at the storm, willing at it with a feeling of his own aliveness. He grips the gunwale as the panga rides an alpine wave. The panga nearing the summit and he lifts his head and looks out from the wave-top. What he sees is a world whirled into being, a world beyond man, a chaotic and empty fury. The wind whips smoke off the wave-top and he bends into his knees as the boat crests the wave then begins its lurch downward.

*

In flashing darkness Bolivar continues to bail. He checks again the rain barrel. Crawls to the front of the boat. It is then by lightning flash he sees the net is gone. He casts his hands about. What remains of the net is a wave-torn shred upon the bitt. He begins to roar, bends and bails with furious strokes. Another flash and Bolivar sees Hector's idol under the stern seat. Something ferocious and occult in its wiry disarray as it returns to darkness, its shape imprinted on the eye. He is overcome by some ill-feeling of a curse. When the effigy comes to be again by lightning strobe Bolivar grabs it and hurls it overboard. He climbs back into the cooler and rests his stinging eyes.

What days have passed, Bolivar does not know. The living self coming out of the shell of the surviving self. How time again opens outward. He climbs out of the cooler with stung-shut eyes, stands blinking, rubs at crusts of salt on the skin. Then he unscrews the top of the rain barrel and dips a cup and takes a drink. He holds the water in his mouth, runs it against the teeth.

Staring at the sky as though he cannot believe.

Two birds beating smoothly the still air.

He turns to see Hector climbing out of the cooler. The youth's eyes are swollen shut. He feels his way with his hands, the skin completely yellow. Bolivar dips the cup and puts it into the outreached hand. Hector takes a long drink. Then he puts down the cup and without word begins to feel under the seat. Then he stops. He fingertips water and wets his eyes and tries to see. His hands begin to move in frantic gestures. He searches the entire boat. Then he stops upon his knees, lifts his head and lets out a wail.

She is gone, he says.

Bolivar stands staring at the lids of the eyes inflamed around the yellowed sight.

Who is gone?

The Virgin.

Hector pulls himself onto the seat and clasps his hands to his face.

I knew this would happen, he says. I began to test her. No wonder she abandoned us. Now we are truly alone.

Then Hector begins to sob. Bolivar watching for a moment. Then he stands up and claps his hands, lets loose a mocking laugh at the sky.

That was some storm! Hey? A real ship killer. But we are not dead yet. Here we are, alive and well. Wait till they hear back home.

Hector turns suddenly with a profound and searching look. What is in the look silences Bolivar. He sees the sickness beneath the lashed skin. The sickness as it rests in the yellowed eyes and cankered mouth. The lids of the eyes inflamed around the yellowed sight. The bones that press through the yellowed skin.

Hector shakes his head.

He says, I see now this was meant to be. There is no

escape. I do not know what I did to deserve this fate but I will face it alone.

Bolivar screws his face at Hector.

Face what alone? Heh? What are you talking about?

He pulls the youth by the elbow.

He says, look, brother. We are in this together. We will figure something out. One thing and then another. We will make another net. We can use the bamboo stick. You will see.

Hector sits and shakes his head.

No, he says. It is fate.

The beating sun sparks off the ocean. Then the current ceases. Bolivar listening carefully to the water. How the ocean seems to forget itself, speaks now almost without breath. The heat in the mouth and how it makes the breath stop, the chest rising and falling in a reflex of breathing without air.

They hide from the sun in the cooler.

In the evening Bolivar lies out over the waters with the bamboo stick. Now and again he turns and studies Hector who sits knees-to-chin within the cooler and does not leave. The yellowed eyes watching something inward. The mouth moving in prayer.

Bolivar's face wrinkles with disgust. He rolls his mouth with an instinct to spit then carefully swallows.

He studies Hector again, then shakes his head.

He thinks, he just won't.

Why won't he?

He closes his eyes and sees the yellowed youth as he sits within his self-made solitude.

He is wrong and I am right.

Bolivar jabs at some darkening twist-shape and misses.

You try to speak to a man's mind. His way of thinking. A man listens or does not listen and if he won't, why is it he won't? What is the won't in a man's mind? What is the won't in *his* mind?

He pulls in a glob of sinuous seaweed and loosens from it dead crabs. He tastes and chews dryly on the algae. Watches a lone seabird that might be a fulmar. The meat underwing and how the bird lands plump upon a broken image.

He stands a moment watching then bends with the stick to the deep.

Why is it he won't?

What he sees in the waters or thinks he can see.

Far below, the shadow of a school writhing like the twistings of a man's mind.

For days now the boat is still. Bolivar with a T-shirt tied over his head, his legs spread out, his mind mugged by heat. Watching the sky held by the sea, ivory upon the waters. Then he sees a farthermost glinting. He is certain it is a ship. He turns towards Hector but does not speak.

For hours, its slow vanishing.

The dead air tastes of salt. Bolivar picks at a scab on his knee and chews it. Then he spits it out. The dead skin too has a salt taste. He runs a finger along the trim and stares at the salt crystals gathered on the skin. His eyes falling upon the sea. He stares into the water. Thought reaching down into the cooling deep until thought swims free. What he holds in his distant look are the tree-tops rising and falling. The bowing green trees as you arrive upon the strip. The leaves of the trees in their wind-breathing green. But the salt air dissolves all things. It dissolves the trees on the strip. It dissolves the strip. The jungled hill and the town are dissolving. The people in the town. Briefly he can see their faces, the places that hold them, and then he cannot.

He grows afraid.

He begins to think he will not remember any of this. It is as if the salt is eating into the place that holds the image. He moves then towards the mountains. He follows the road from the town to where she lives.

Alexa.

He tries to see the house. But the salt dissolves the road. It dissolves the house. He steps through the door into the room and sees the salt dissolving her skin. The air around her skin. It dissolves her voice.

He listens.

He listens through the dissolving image as though to discern some faraway whisper. He listens until he can hear the dissolved voice trembling, the voice speaking to him. What it says.

You did not know you loved.

✽

A bird rides the evening zephyr. When the bird clips along the hull Bolivar follows soft-foot behind. The head twitching this way and that. Black cap and orange bill. It looks like some kind of tern, maybe. The flutter and then furling wing. It is then that Bolivar finds himself moving through the air, finds his hands at the bird's throat. Hector's yellowed eyes watching in disgust as Bolivar fights the bird with blood-pecked hands then skins it. He complains when Bolivar slices the meat off the breast and thighs. Then he climbs out of the cooler and sits with a sorrowful look.

He says, you cannot eat that.

Bolivar says, why not?

It is a sin.

Bolivar stops with the knife.

How is it a sin?

It is not food. It is not clean.

How is this not food?

Bolivar turns muttering and shakes his head. Then he twists the knife into the meat, cuts a piece and slides it off the blade into his mouth. The youth's face puckers in disgust and his teeth flash as Bolivar slowly rolls the taste. He stares at the youth who suddenly looks away. Then Bolivar swallows and his mouth shrinks with distaste. He takes a small drink of water and smiles.

It is very oily, he says. It tastes of rotten fish. But you are what you eat, no?

Hector does not answer.

Bolivar leans closer to him.

You are getting sick. Really, you should eat some.

*

Hector watches Bolivar now with a yellowed sneering look. One bird and then another. How with two quick motions he leaves each bird shorn of its wings, pens them with driftwood into the bow. Stands over the birds and calls them chickens. When it is time to kill, Bolivar slices the meat into portions and puts them to soften in brine. Hector drinks water but refuses to eat. In hunger the birds begin to peck at each other, to call through the night and the day in their squawkings, Hector growing more and more aghast as their faeces litter the hull. He shifts about, he cannot sleep, lies with his hands over his ears. He takes the bamboo spear and tries to fish with it, stabs uselessly at the water. Then some dark fish takes the spear in its back and Hector whoops but the fish pulls the spear free of his hand. He watches it pass into the waters. Stands wringing his hands, Bolivar stamping about the boat in a rage. Then he stands before Hector with his hands on his hips and shouts at him. It is just like you to do that. As he turns the boat makes a sudden lurch. Bolivar looks up to see Hector moving swiftly down the boat, the youth taking a cup of bird meat and throwing it overboard. He cups with two hands a wingless bird and tosses it over the trim, reaches for another.

With a roar Bolivar is upon Hector. He grabs the youth by the nose and throat, Hector with his head thrust back, he is beating an arm up and down upon Bolivar as though trying to take flight. Then he reaches with a thumb and hooks Bolivar in the mouth.

In silence they grapple among the scattering birds, the panga swaying upon the even sea, Bolivar sensing now the weakness within Hector's body, an infirmity in the limbs, the spent and wheezing breath. He can sense too his own power. He shapes Hector into a headlock and twists pressure, mutters coarsely into his ear.

What are you? You are nothing—

Some feeling of might and justice surging through the blood, squeezing as Hector ceases to struggle.

It is then that Bolivar lets the youth drop.

Hector falls bent onto his knees sucking with great serrations on his breath, his eyes popped-out. Then he fixes upon Bolivar a wounded and hateful look. He crawls towards the cooler and begins to sob. Bolivar keeping watch before turning to survey his birds.

He begins to pull at his beard, sits down with great shakings of his hands, stands up again.

He turns and roars at Hector.

It makes no difference to me whether you die or not. You can die all you like out here. But destroy my food? Take away my chance? That is a crime. I will kill you for that. I will tear out your eyes.

For days Bolivar moves about the boat around an unwilling and wordless Hector. Then the youth climbs out of the cooler, stands very still, calls to Bolivar in a reluctant voice. Bolivar pretends not to hear, lies spread out under sheeting, chewing on a rind of toe-nail. Hector calls again in half-whisper. He raises slowly a crooked hand and points. Bolivar lifts the sheeting and watches the youth rapt it seems by some vision. He drops the sheeting and climbs out of it. Watches with narrowed eyes.

The ocean in fields of final light.

Then within the half-sun an image.

He closes his eyes and opens them. It is as though something had been burnt into his retina.

Something huge and slow and darkened.

It cannot be—

His voice cracks.

Then he says, it is coming our way.

They watch a container ship come to be.

Hector turns with a fearful look.

Do you think they have seen us?

Bolivar begins to move. He looks for something to wave, grabs hold of a bleached-orange plastic bag, ties it to the plank.

He says, they have seen us, for sure.

He begins to wave the plank and shout.

They watch the ship cruise towards them.

Then Hector shakes his head.

He says, it is really going to happen.

They jump and wave and cheer with torn voices. They come to see a great tonnage of coloured containers stacked seven-high upon the deck. Bolivar studying the bridge hundreds of feet above the ocean. Not a person to be seen. A sudden ripple of fear passing through his body as the ship's hum carries through the water. What he begins to see is something unremitting in the ship's fixed intent. They watch as it comes upon them. They watch and each man comes to know it. They stand then within that knowing. They stand and feel the passing breath of the ship as it shuts out the sky. Then the panga goes dark within the ship's faceless expression. Hector's face turns wretched. The men scream and shout and wave their flag but the ship carries onwards without a sailor in sight. It passes into shadow. Passes into the night. Hector a rucked shape pulling at his hair. Bolivar pinching the cords of his throat.

He lifts his head to stare into what has just happened. The ship as it was. The ship nevermore.

Bolivar watches Hector sitting in a ball and he looks at the sea and he looks at his own sun-browned skin. It is then it comes upon him, a quaking laughter that rises from some deep unknown. Hector turns with a mute shudder. Bolivar would like to stop, he pulls at his hair, he shakes his head, he slaps his thighs, but the laughter continues to come. Then Hector stands up. He moves towards Bolivar and fixes him with a rancorous look. His hands curl and his eyes seem to spit out of his face.

Then finally he speaks in a plain, factual tone.

It is your fault.

Bolivar stares into the eyes that sit now as though dead in the speaking face. It is then he stops laughing.

Hector says, they saw what you had. Your little zoo of birds. They could see you for what you are. A cruel and twisted man. I have always known it. Letting the birds live like that without wings. Such a sight before God. They would have heard the screeching for sure. They watched you in their binoculars and they said, that there is a sicko, take a good look at him, he goes to sea to torment birds, he pulls off their wings and lets them live in agony and distress until he eats them, he is among the damned for sure. And so they passed by. So you see, Bolivar, it is your fault. Nothing is of any use now. I had an opportunity to go home, to catch her doing those things she has been doing behind my back. And now she will never know that I know.

Bolivar stares at Hector's yellowed teeth, at the eyes vanishing into the caves of the skull.

He thinks, he is losing his mind. He is growing old. It is now an old man's face, for sure.

Hector's black pebble eyes. He seems no longer aware of Bolivar, has sat for days within stillness, his eyes unseeing yet open. Bolivar watching the youth. He tries to see what might be in the youth's mind but cannot. Sometimes he can hear Hector whispering some prayer. Bolivar cuts bird meat into strips and lays it on the cowling to cook. Their water is getting low but sooner or later, he knows, this humid weather will give rain. He studies the flats of sea and sky. Then he sees it, a giant bird. He squints at it a long time. He is sure it is an albatross, the bird white on darkened wings is expertly motionless. He tells Hector to look but the youth does not stir.

At sundown he goes for a hobbled run. His sun-browned back grown crooked. The knees arthritic, the elbows protruding, the lungs buckling under the body's weight. His mind watching himself as he once was on the strip. The body firm and upright upon the beach. The blood circulating. The body supple and proceeding and automatic in what it does. The flesh alert and tasting the air. He can see himself moving by the panga on the strip. There is Hector alongside Arturo walking towards him. He is watching Hector's flimsy body, his long arms and legs, his inner being projecting outward some kind of sickness of spirit, that is what it is, a great not-doing within him. A man cannot become some other man. You are made of what is in you.

Bolivar stops running and leans at the edge of the cooler fighting for breath. He can see Hector inside, whispering himself into being, he has not moved today.

It is then he finds himself shouting in Hector's face.

Look, Hector! A ship!

Hector does not stir at Bolivar's mocking laughter.

Bolivar now within a rage. He juts his face within an inch of Hector's yellowed skin, the quarried lips, the rotten breath. The edgeless, calm indifference.

He shouts, what is wrong with you? You need to wake up! You need to eat! How many times have I told you to take heart? Why won't you listen?

He grabs Hector by the shoulder and shakes him.

Hector lifts his head and fixes a blank stare upon Bolivar. Then he shuts his eyes and rests within. When he opens them again a glimmer of something stirs in the eyes as though a thought has come into being, the thought resting there, growing in its own light. Then Hector's mouth opens. He speaks in a resigned and distant voice.

Something is growing within my body. It is like weight, only different. It is always there now. It is growing within me. I can feel it here.

Bolivar watches the finger point to the chest.

He goes to speak but falls silent.

He rubs his hands and looks up.

Look, brother. You just need to eat. That's all there is to it.

Hector says, yes, I am hungry. I will eat some fish.

But there is no fish.

It is OK. I know what you did.

What is OK?

What you have done.

What do you mean, what I have done?

You have been hiding the fish from me all this time, eating it at night.

Bolivar's mouth falls open.

But there is no fish. We lost our net in the—

I want you to believe it is OK, Bolivar.

No, it is not OK!

Listen, I forgive you.

Hey! I haven't done anything.

Bolivar stands before him grinding his teeth, his hands squeezing open and shut. He stares at his fists.

Hector smiles and closes his eyes.

Into black night Bolivar wakes. He pads his hand to where Hector should be, sits suddenly up. What his mind sees. Hector sliding himself into the water that wraps around him his grave. With quickness then he is moving out of the cooler. There is Hector on his knees, the skin thinly etched by moonlight, the face lifted towards the night. The sound of whispered prayer. Then Hector stops. He is aware now of Bolivar and rests back on his heels. A moment later, he speaks.

Did you know, Bolivar, that we are already dead? I'll bet you didn't know this. But it is a fact.

Bolivar's mouth goes dry. He tries to speak but no words come out. He rests a hand against the cooler, stands very still sensing the air between them, sensing the silence that rests in the air, sensing what rests in the silence.

Hector says, we died during that first storm. I died that time I fell in. I did not even notice. The line of life and death. How strange and slim it is. It is something we do not experience. Just a simple passing through. You come up out of the water gasping for air not knowing you are already dead. It is so simple. And now we are here, adrift in this place. You see, Bolivar, this is neither heaven nor hell. That is our punishment. We have been cast out. We lost sight of God. Now we are being taught what not seeing him truly means. Not seeing. Never seeing. Never will see. Maybe always not. This is what absence truly is. It must be met as suffering.

Hector falls silent. He pulls his hair out of his face.

A moment later, he begins to speak.

Maybe now this means it is OK she is with him. This is what I am thinking over and over. She has given herself over to sinning while I have the sinning thoughts. And so I see how all this has been designed for me.

Bolivar stares at what forms Hector in the dark. The dark that clads the body and brings the body into itself. The body mysterious and only the hair and face traced by moonlight, the words he speaks that trace the being, the ulcered mouth he can imagine seeing as it twists the words, the yellow eyes believing what the mouth says.

Bolivar does not know what to say.

He tries to speak but no words come out.

Finally he clears his throat.

Look, he says, we can still figure this out. I have spent how many years doing this— I don't know. Ten years, maybe. All this time at sea has hardened my bones. We can still do it. I intend to see us through. I am the captain of this ship. We have the rest of our lives ahead of us.

The voice before him seems to issue in whisper without body as though born of the darkness itself.

You do not understand, Bolivar. It is much too late. The true nature of your own fate is for you to discover. Maybe the punishment designed for you is that you must face the abandonment you created. You will never again see her, your child. Yes, I see this now.

It is then that Bolivar rushes towards Hector, grabs hold of him, begins to shake him.

Then he stops and lets him go.

Hector does not speak.

Without word Bolivar climbs back into the cooler.

Bolivar sits pinching the bridge of his nose. He watches a band of shelved cloud form maybe thirty, forty miles away. The sky become haze. He sees again an albatross rolling the high air without beating its wings. He fixes the rain cups and senses the temperature drop. Hector has hardly moved since he returned to the cooler. He does not move now when the wind carries the rain over the waters. Bolivar moving about the boat, keeping watch over the cups and the barrel, keeping watch over Hector. He is an insect again, he thinks. You do not know what an insect might do. He faces into the rain and stands as though fetching some faraway thought. Feeling the rain on his skin, stretching out his arms, lost for a moment in its touch.

They ride rough sea for two days. Sleep now heaving upon violent dreams. Then in sleep Bolivar hears Alexa sing. He is trying to move towards her, his legs trying to flee the boat, he is trying to climb out but cannot – his legs are dead, the blood thickened by salt, his voice hoarse and yet he manages to shout, I am coming! I am coming! He wakes into darkness and meets his own self. He listens and hears the sea grown calm.

There is only this, he thinks. You cannot move past this. Do not listen to him. Nothing he says is. What does he want? He does not want. It is not wanting that he wants. That is the problem. His mind is being twisted by the sickness in the body.

Bolivar listens until he can hear himself as he shouted in the dream.

I am coming!

It is then he hears it. Some distant ululation passing through the waters.

He thinks, maybe it is a whale singing, who knows.

He listens and again he hears it.

He whispers to himself.

Do not worry, Alexa, I hear you. For sure, I am coming back.

Flying fish break the waters. He watches as they soar outstretched towards the sun then make their plummeting fall.

He wakes to the nearby scuffling of a bird. His breathing stops, his mind passing from dream into the cooler, the cold and beyond. He moves onto his elbow and listens. It is then he finds his body leaping, his hands meeting the body of some hulked bird, the creature screeching, smashing its wings, moving with unexpected torque to strike with its beak at his face and hands. He fights until the bird falls quiet.

He watches the east grow in a cold furnace of light. Sees that what he has killed is an albatross. He looks at his bleeding hands.

He skins the bird and cuts it open. The insides are full of undigested plastic. He slices some breast meat and puts it into brine. He watches Hector carefully when he wakes, the way Hector sits, where the eyes rest, the sunken chest, one shoulder higher than the other. Hector has not bothered to lift his head.

Bolivar thinks, nobody would believe it, but it is easier at sea to catch birds than fish.

In the days that pass Hector does not speak. He slumps in the cooler, the hands folded and faintly worrying as though spirit were something hands could wring. Bolivar studying the hands, the dry mouth, the feeling that the youth's being is withdrawing to someplace else. He puts water to Hector's lips and the water spills down the chin. Bolivar continues to speak to Hector as though nothing has altered. He explains aloud his dreams. He remembers events from his childhood. He says, the day my grandfather disappeared. I can still recall it. Later, he says, it is strange, you know, but my hearing is getting so good I can hear things passing beneath us in the water. I can see things clearly that are far away.

Later, he steps behind the cooler and washes the albatross meat. He tastes a small cut. It is oily, he thinks, but it does not taste of dead fish.

He chews quietly watching the horizon, the depthless waters in meeting with it. The mind reaching and false before both, he thinks. And yet both false before the mind.

He finds himself before Hector with a piece of meat cut into thin strips.

Look, he says, I caught a fish.

Hector lifts his head to look.

Bolivar says, I don't know what kind it is.

Hector raises his fingers crooked before the offering. He takes the meat and puts it in his mouth and chews.

Bolivar watching him as he eats, the ulcers on the lips and tongue, the gums bleeding onto the food.

Bolivar says, full belly, happy heart.

Hector looks up and smiles without expression.

Yes, he says. It is a nice piece of fish.

He eats another piece then falls silent.

Then he says, can I have a taste of water? For days my tongue is burning.

Hector moans himself awake. There is something within the moan that disturbs Bolivar. He turns to see Hector lying in an agonised curl. His hands clutching his gut. His brow wet with fever. He has vomited what little food he has eaten. Quickly Bolivar goes to lift him but Hector shrugs away the help. He crawls as though with great weight out of the cooler and curls against the hull, lies there a wretched shape, Bolivar watching, pulling at his hair. He bends over the boat and wets a hand in the sea, washes Hector's brow. He moves the long hair out of the youth's eyes, washes the crud off the lips. He sees that Hector has soiled himself. He takes a cup and washes him. Then he lifts Hector out of the sun and puts him in the cooler.

He keeps Hector's brow cool, puts drink to the lips. He tries to keep him warm at night. It seems to him that Hector's bones are writhing under the skin. The lips whispering veiled and innermost words.

Bolivar stares with suspicion at the meat.

You are not sick, he thinks. It did you no harm, it is some other thing. Look at his skin, he is completely yellow, his blood must be poisoned.

Bolivar takes a sniff of the albatross meat. He takes a little bite. It is fine, he thinks.

He throws the meat overboard.

Day into night and night into day. How many days, three or four, he isn't sure, but Hector begins to breathe calmly in sleep. Then he wakes and sits up. He stares at Bolivar who watches the youth and sees that something has changed within his expression. Bolivar studies the skin drawn yellow over the bones. The thin beard hanging past the chin. The hair past the shoulders and how it palls the eyes. How the youth sits for a long time with an absent, benevolent look. Then he seems to smile.

Bolivar holds out food but Hector pushes it away.

He leans forward and puts a hand to the youth's shoulder, gently shakes him.

You have to eat, brother.

I am past that now.

What do you mean?

Hector does not answer.

Bolivar stares into the smile that leads into the mouth. He stares into the mouth that leads into the mind that spoke the words. He stares as though he can see into the words but he cannot. What he sees is some faraway thought vanishing on the youth's face.

He grabs Hector and shakes hurt into the youth's shoulder, Hector's hair falling loose across the eyes.

Bolivar shouts, what are you smiling for?

He rushes then, goes to the cups and grabs at some

other bird meat, stuffs it into Hector's mouth, the long
hair tangling with the food, Bolivar holding his hand over
the youth's mouth trying to force him to swallow, holding
the hand tight against the mouth as though trying to—

He stops, stares at his hand.

Hector calmly pulls the hair out of his mouth.

He spits the food into his palm and hands it back to
Bolivar. He begins to smile again but something lies dead
within the eyes as though the place in the mind that holds
the thought cannot meet the light.

Hector says, why don't you see, Bolivar?

Bolivar stares at Hector with horror.

What he sees in the youth's expression is joy.

The wind leaps from south-east to north. A sudden rain
fills their cups. Then days of white heat. A jet stream high
above strews the long wake of a ship. The sun clocking
around Hector where he sits unmoved. Bolivar watching how the youth holds within him some strange and
immense self-possession. His hands on his knees, a faint
smile on the lips. He is still refusing to eat. Bolivar watching the youth's body. How the skin seems to hang less
taut each day. He thinks, the muscle for sure is being
devoured from within, the skin meeting bone, the mind
devouring the body. He studies the youth for sign of the
will within. He watches the youth and falls into a doze.
Sees him again inside a dream, Hector smiling at him, the
youth's skin beginning to shimmer in the hazed evening
light, the body trembling, the body it seems beginning to

move apart from the body, the body becoming double in his vision – he tries to wake from the dream, his eyes still fixed upon Hector, for sure the youth is breaking in two, he is trying to break free from the body—

Bolivar wakes with a start.

He stares with suspicion at Hector but the youth has not moved.

A small green turtle butts the boat. Bolivar wrestles it out of the water and carefully drains the blood into a cup. He portions the organ meat, holds the liver quivering in his hand.

He says, really, you must eat some.

He turns to look at Hector and sees the youth weeping into the crook of his arm.

Bolivar turns away as Hector looks up.

He says, it is a great pity, Bolivar, that we met at the end of our lives.

Bolivar turns upon Hector.

Hey! Stop with this crazy talk, eh?

He wipes from his mouth the mess of bloodied liver, rests a blood-smeared hand on Hector's shoulder.

We are still young, he says. We have our whole lives ahead of us.

I wanted to be like you, Bolivar. I thought I could be like you. I tried to do as you do. The way you move about the boat. The way you move your hands. The way you think. You are so good at this. But I cannot be like you. I cannot change who I am.

Look, this is no time to give in. You must have faith.

Hector slowly lifts his head and stares at Bolivar, the face screened by hair, and yet Bolivar can see the wet yellowed eyes take on a sudden look of severity, the mouth pulling into sneer.

All I have left is my faith.

Bolivar pulls his hand back from Hector's shoulder, turns the hand open and stares at it.

Yes, maybe. But you do not have faith in this. What we are doing. You do not believe. You are a *no*, not a *yes*.

It is you, Bolivar, who is a *no*, not a *yes*. It is you who does not believe.

Hey. That is not true. Somebody is coming for us, wait till you see.

It is you who refuses to see.

What days pass. Bolivar watching at the length of his vision, alert to every moving thing. The remote sea giving things up. What looks like the flashing of a signal. A distant ship in silhouette. A maelstrom of seabirds swarming some bloated dead thing. He listens to the shadows that pass beneath the boat. His hands ready to pull from the water a shark if one should surface and draw close.

He tries to fish with a plastic bag.

Again and again he tells himself, you will find a fish, you will find a fish and make him eat. You can save him yet.

He sees in his mind Hector as he once was, then stares at the youth wasting away. Hector within the body yet not of the body. The eyes fixed on something inward. The body pulling inward as though following what the mind sees, the mind seeking something within.

He can see that Hector has aged greatly. What sits before him now is the spent body of an old man. The ankles and feet swollen.

He begins to examine his own body, pulls at loose skin. It is now a deep leathery brown but not the youth's shrunken yellow. He looks at his hands and feet and wonders if his face has changed.

He leans over the boat and tries to see his face on the water. The face before him an inconstant fluid thing. It is the face Alexa must see in her dreams. He thinks about her face as she once was. Who she could be now. He touches his cheeks. She will not recognise you. She will not believe who you are.

He holds his face in his hands and weeps.

Slowly Hector opens his mouth as though to speak.

A tooth falls out.

Bolivar sits in the cooler chewing the last of the turtle meat. He offers some to Hector who does not look at him. Then Bolivar leans out of the panga and scoops water, carries it in his hands. He washes Hector's face, wipes the hair out of the eyes, wipes the brow. The skin is clammy and cold. He puts his arms around the youth and tries to warm him. He is trying not to let Hector see he is weeping again. Hector's eyes closed now for what seems like days.

Bolivar finds himself shouting at him.

You cannot do this. You must wake up.

He pushes himself away from Hector, walks up and down the boat in a rage, then goes for a run.

He wakes in the middle of the night and hears himself roar, you are behaving like a fool. You need to wake from this thing.

He finds himself upon his knees begging Hector to listen. He pulls at his arm.

Look, why won't you look? If you think this is a dream then it is you who are dreaming. You can do this. You can wake up. I know you can do it. I really know it. I need you to do it for me. You cannot leave me here on my own.

Bolivar goes for a run around the cooler then stops breathless, crouches against the hull. A long time just watching. The making and unmaking of the sea in some sourceless ancient reflex. What are you? How a body can part the waters but never a thought. A thought can move the body to part the waters but the waters never meet the thought. He studies a seabird black and solitary against the sun. The bird spirals then planes towards the panga. He sees a red sac at the throat. It is a frigate bird and it pulls its long black wings into its body as it lands on the trim.

Bolivar places it staggering and wingless in the aviary.

Hector begins to weep. He sits with the mouth parted as though searching for the right words. The lids of the eyes are swollen. Then he points for a drink of water. Bolivar puts a cup to the youth's lips.

As he drinks, a shiver suddens through Hector's body.

His eyes meet Bolivar's eyes with a strange and pure expression. Then he speaks, his voice barely a whisper.

I have not lived well, Bolivar.

Bolivar sits with a sad and frowning face.

That is not true. How can that be true?

I have been a burden, to you, to others. There are many ill-doings I must account for.

What are you talking about? You are not some murderer, a car thief or something.

All these small things I have been doing. They add up. I am the sum of all this. I can feel this now. This is what has been growing inside me. I can feel it here in my chest. It is a feeling that is greater than any pain in my body. Every ill-doing I can see before me now. I have not been a good person. So I am spending this time remembering. I am revisiting each action. I can see myself back there as I am doing each thing. I see the action and I experience pain when I see it. I have not been kind to my mother and father. My sister and brother. I have not been kind to Lucrezia, that is for sure. It is no wonder she has run away with him.

Look, Hector, you have no idea what she has done.

The only thing left for me to do is to seek forgiveness for each action. I have been thinking that we create our own fate. This is so, Bolivar, don't you think? Every single thing you do takes you to where you are now and not any other place. This can only be so. But every deed you do gives rise to a feeling inside you. So we are what we have done. This is what I think. We are accountable because we act upon what we feel. I think I understand this now. Maybe not. Maybe this is not how it is. But I feel this to be true. I have not been kind to you, Bolivar. I am sorry about this. There have been many times when I let you down. Will you forgive me? Will you be kind in your memory towards me?

Bolivar sits trying not to listen. He puts his hands over his ears, then his face. He stares at his hands and wills himself to believe. He can see a ship coming to be on the waters, pulling up alongside the panga. He can see a red plane coming low over the waves. It is a seaplane. He is climbing inside it. He is going straight to Rosa's place with a foil blanket on his shoulders. Hector is with him. This is what happens. You have seen this on TV. Angel beside you. Rosa holding your hand. Everyone leaning in to listen. Everybody offering you a drink.

He thinks, it is not the body that is the problem. The problem is the mind.

Hector says, she is with him now. She is in his car and they are driving about. I can see them. It is a nice day, a little humid maybe. She is happy. They are caught up in their lives, in the doing of each thing. It is the doing that makes us forget ourselves. She will not notice I am gone.

Hector bows his head and lets loose a sob that shakes his body. Then he speaks in a low voice.

I did not pass fully through. I see this now. The self must be rid of the weight within it before there can be a passing through.

He closes his eyes and stops talking.

Bolivar tries to keep Hector warm with body heat and blanketing seaweed. He tells him things about himself of which he has never spoken. Regrets from an older life. He speaks to him about his daughter.

He says, I'm trying to figure out, Hector, what day you will begin to eat. So we can tell them back home. Is it this day or tomorrow? Isn't that right, Hector, it was today you began to eat and get well again.

Bolivar cuts some bird meat and tastes it. He tries to wake Hector but he does not stir. Bolivar shakes him. He begins to shout.

What right have you to do this? You have no right. I will kill you first before you die. I will kill you in your sleep.

Then Bolivar sits in the cooler, puts his head in his hands and weeps.

I am sorry, my friend, he says. I do not know what I am saying.

He lifts Hector carefully into a sitting position, puts an ear to his chest. It is difficult to hear if Hector is breathing or not.

Bolivar wakes to primrose light. The panga pitching on a south-westerly swell. He says aloud, we are really moving on the water today. We have turned again. Now we are pointing north-east by north.

Hector does not answer.

Bolivar tries fishing with the plastic bag. Then he crouches before Hector. He tries to remember what day it was when Hector last spoke. He can see the parched skin is now a dying colour. He leans closer until he can see a semblance of the life force under the skin.

A faint pulse beneath the ribs. A flicker in the throat. A trembling in the tissue upon the eyelids.

He stares at Hector's closed eyes and folded hands. He believes he can see the mind willing against the life force. The self willing against that which gives it being.

He thinks, he belongs here. He is a part of all this. He is a part of you. The way he sits in this space. The light as it rests upon the body. The shadow made by the body. That is his also. The salt on the skin. The salt must rest on something, it rests on him.

Bolivar finds himself shaking Hector.

Hey! Wake up! Come on, will you. Let's go for a run.

He pulls Hector out of the cooler and swings him onto his back. Then he begins to run around the cooler. Quickly his chest grows tight. He falls onto his knees and drops Hector beside him. The youth begins to stir a little. He whispers faint words, lies watching Bolivar with skulled eyes that give a pensive, sorrowful look.

Bolivar claps his hands and says, you are awake! What would you like for breakfast? I can make you some eggs.

Hector slowly blinks.

Bolivar puts Hector back in the cooler. He sits hoping for some sign of the living will within Hector. Wishing it to rise and renew. But what he sees is winter light, the will in repose, the will prevailing barely in the awry breathing, the will withdrawn and acquiescent to something else being unwilled deep within.

What is told in the eyes.

Bolivar stands up and slaps his hands together.

Maybe I'll kill a chicken for dinner.

Hector slowly lifts an arm. He reaches out a hand for Bolivar who steps towards him and gives Hector his wrist. Hector grips the wrist for a long time. Then he tries to lean forward. Bolivar helps him into a sit.

An old smile alights the youth's eyes.

He speaks in whisper.

Bolivar, you are my greatest friend.

Bolivar sits alone watching the dusk sea. He sees a distant diving whale. The tail taking the shape of a soaring bird, water dripping off vanishing wings.

The sea without sun. Bolivar covers Hector with seaweed and rises. He beats his arms about his chest, rubs his legs and stretches, begins to run. He half-closes his eyes. He is running from the strip. He is running over back roads towards the hills and then he is running the rutted hill road, the air is dusty here, you have a long way to go, it is good that you came with food.

He thinks, she will not remember you now, a long time has passed, it is ten years or so. You will have to wash your face before you go, clean your nails, wear a nice shirt, speak a few words to her mother, tell her, look, isn't it better I came back a repentant man than not at all? I was a weakling back then for sure.

The joints of his knees creak and there is a low-pitched complaint in his bones. He stops and leans upon the trim and bends into the wheezing breath. In the sky behind he can sense the air whispering two birds, knows from their path and call they have seen the boat. He turns then and sees two black-footed albatrosses begin to circle the boat.

He goes to Hector and shakes him gently by the shoulder.

Hey! Wake up. Are you hungry today? I have some smoked fish. You look very cold. It is OK, I will let you sleep a while longer.

Later, he tries again to rouse Hector.

Hey! Hector, it is time for you to wake! I have prepared for us a great dinner, all types of things, the very best, all the things you like.

Hey! Why won't you wake?

He sits watching the wind, how it passes over the water.

During the day Bolivar lifts Hector out of the cooler and sits him against the hull. At night he lays him in the cooler, arranges his arms and legs, asks if he is comfortable. Then he climbs in and wraps his arms around him and sleeps. What he dreams. A dark and tunnelling black until he dreams he is Hector, Hector trapped within some dead dream of things that used to be. Bolivar wakes screaming.

He lies then unable to sleep, listening to the sea. The moon laid out, ashen upon the hull.

He weeps as he carries Hector gently from the cooler. Weeps as he props him against the hull, arranges the arms and legs. Look, Hector, I have some chicken for you to eat. It is the loveliest day. Look at the sun, it is having a low day, for sure, but still you must see it. I wish I had the words to explain how lovely it is. It is a kind of lemon colour. You can see the same colour glistening on the water. I know you are sick of seeing these things, but still, the world is very beautiful. If only everyone could see this.

Bolivar tries to eat food but cannot. He watches the weather. Looking and looking until he cannot see what is seen. He tries to fish with bare hands. Then he just sits. A voice from long ago whispers a song and he begins to hum under the breath. It is a song he has not heard since childhood. The words come half-remembered and he sings along, tears falling down his face.

He sits talking aloud. He still cannot eat. He takes a few small sips of rainwater and rinses his mouth then swallows.

He says, we are running out of water again.

Then he says, I thought you were some sort of insect. What do you think of that? Now you are my closest friend. How strange life is, no? It is always trying to trick you. To make you do the wrong thing.

Do you know, the first thing I will do when I get home is I will go see my daughter. Then I will go see Rosa. Or maybe I will see Rosa first because I will have to return to the strip. Maybe those animal urges will return to my body. It has been a long time. She will be happy to see me, for sure. Then I will go see Alexa. I will be calm, yes, very calm going to visit her. Maybe Rosa will come with me, she will help, she will know what to do.

Look, Hector, I think you have made a bet. I think you have made the biggest bet that can be made on this earth. But I have made a different bet and I will prove you wrong. You will see, it is going to happen.

The sun rounds and rounds again. He sleeps or does not sleep, he does not know. He sits and watches his hands shaking. He grabs hold of Hector and shouts, this is all your fault, not mine! Then he turns upon himself, shouts at his hands to be still. He sobs uncontrollably, closes his eyes and slumps against the hull.

When he wakes he begins to scream, whirls with flailing arms upon seabirds that sit feeding on Hector's face.

The birds flurry and flutter upward then settle on the sea.

Bolivar staring at Hector's pecked-out eyes.

He begins to pull his own hair.

He says, I am so sorry, Hector. I am so sorry about this. It is all my fault. I was not looking out for you. Please forgive me.

He lifts Hector like a child and holds him to his chest. He cries and yells at the sky. Then he begins to curse himself. You are an ignorant fool. A buffoon. A simpleton. You should never have been born. You are not good enough to have even been a fisherman.

He sits still for a long time. He thinks he sleeps. When he wakes, Hector is still in his arms. The sea and the sky unbinding with light. He studies Hector's face. The skin has relaxed and taken on a grey pallor. The trace of a smile on the lips.

Bolivar stares, unbelieving.

What is this? he says.

He drops Hector and storms about the boat.

He stands over Hector and shouts.

Look! I have had enough of this. I know you are not dead. So please, stop pretending.

He shakes Hector, drops him again and continues to shout.

I am better off without you. You have been nothing but trouble since the start. Look at you. You are a waste of life. You could have done so many things. I will tell them what you have done. I will tell them all the trouble you caused me. You are nothing but an insect.

He hauls Hector up by the armpits and reverses against the gunwale. Then with a swing, he lifts Hector over the side of the boat, stands hugging the body.

He cannot let go.

The wind blows Hector's hair into Bolivar's face and he spits the salty hair taste out of his mouth.

He wills himself to let Hector go but his arms remain locked around the body.

Then he screams.

He screams again and lets go.

Scarcely a sound as the body slides into the water.

He stares at his empty hands.

Bolivar lies within the cooler sobbing for his friend. He has forgotten to eat. Now and then he drinks a little water. Watching the shadows fall. Watching the shadows edge across the boat. The shadow as the life force of a thing. This is what he thinks. The life force trying to escape the fate of the thing, the body or the object. The shadow fleeing the barrel, fleeing from the knife. Staring now with horror at what issues from his own body. The shadows fleeing his darkened feet. The shadows fleeing his calves, his knees, his thighs. Soon, he thinks, there will be nothing left.

His hands are wet with sweat. He sits up and leans forward trying to breathe. He climbs out of the cooler, moving with the shadow, heavy and breathless and clutching at his chest. His eyes meet the sea and the sea carries his sight across the wastes of waning light towards some immense and unseen thing. A scream building inside his body. He turns and stares at the empty boat, his chest tightening, he is suddenly dizzy, he grabs onto the trim and sucks air.

For a long time he is afraid to move.

He tells himself not to look out upon the sea.

He looks out and the sea takes the thought to its far-thest reaches until the thought falls inward upon itself.

He finds himself on his knees as though winded, his eyes squeezed against the light. He beats the hull with his fists, roars out Hector's name.

You stupid insect! What have you done? How can you leave me alone?

He pulls himself up, kicks the hull then howls and grabs his foot, hobbles about the boat screaming Hector's name.

He stares fiercely at the dark. Screams at it until his voice is hoarse.

This!

What you have done to me! Goddamn you!

What am I supposed to do now?

He sits against the hull nursing his foot. Then he folds his arms and does not move, sinks within himself.

He tells himself he will sleep like this.

He tells himself if he does not move he will not have to think.

The thought that presses from the darkest place.

What it says.

To stare directly at it. What it might mean.

You are alone.

From blackest sleep Bolivar snaps awake. A hand has touched his elbow. He opens his eyes into airless heat, turns to meet the sun's meridian, his arms, his legs are burning. He senses another in the panga. He sits up bewildered, bats at the sun with his hand. He is searching for the remnants of a dream but there was no dream. He has slept like this, sprawled on the deck, the fierce sun flaming the hull to a dry and polished bone.

His dry tongue searches his mouth.

He climbs onto his knees searching for water.

It is then he sees Hector.

He screams, his hands clawing the air, the scream dying in his mouth. His mind willing the body to move backward but he stands rooted, only his arms can move, the thought screaming through the heavy heated blood.

Hector remains calmly seated by the stern, his hands resting on his lap. He is watching Bolivar with pecked-out eyes.

Hello, Porky.

Bolivar crouches with shut eyes refusing to look. Behind him the screeching aviary. He whispers, you are dreaming with open eyes. He opens his eyes and takes a look then shuts his eyes again.

He whispers, you can will yourself to wake if you do not look.

His hand slides quietly over the knife.

The heat resting in the hull is burning the skin and soles of his feet. He presses his body into the burn and wills the pain to wake him. Slowly, heavily, with shut eyes he sits himself up onto the bow seat. The hot air crawling in his throat. He pulls the knife towards his body. He opens one eye and then another.

There is Hector on the stern seat, his hands now resting with open fingers on the knees, the hair strewn over the face. A faint smile creasing the corners of the lips. He leans forward as though trying to force sight through the pecked-out eyes. Then he leans back.

He says, I know you are there, Porky.

For a long time Bolivar is unable to speak. He sits biting his tongue, staring at Hector as though willing what he sees to belong to a dream he can wake from.

Hector smoothly purses his lips and blows the hair out of his face.

Then he begins to move, his gaunt yellowed body hinging upward, his hand reaching blindly for the gunwale. He follows the trim around the back of the cooler and Bolivar crawls around the opposite side barely able to breathe. He cannot look as Hector feels his way to the bow, Hector bending to the aviary, the sound of teeth tearing into meat, then the sound of water being poured overboard, the sound of the empty barrel being dropped onto the hull.

Then Bolivar can feel Hector turning towards him.

The body moving.

He opens his eyes and waves the knife, roars for Hector to stay back.

What he sees is Hector stopped with a smile, a mess of blood and feathers behind him. Then the youth begins to move towards the cooler where he feels his way in and takes seat. He leans out and stares with blind eyes.

Relax, Porky. I only want to talk.

Bolivar tries to speak, his tongue upon the words but the sound will not come. He forces a dry swallow. Finds a whispered voice.

What are you? Some sort of devil?

The smile falls from Hector's face.

He says, whatever do you mean? I am Hector, your greatest friend.

For a long time Bolivar crouches against the hull willing his eyes upon Hector. He sees in his mind his hands letting go of Hector's body. The body sliding into the water and sinking into the deep. He studies now the ravaged body spread with ease in the cooler. The corrugations of skin over the ribs. The boil gnawing upon the neck.

He takes the knife and pits his own hip with it. Watches the pinprick of blood and tastes it.

He studies the sea.

He tells himself, all this is real.

The heat as it tremors upon the water.

The sun rent upon the water in filament light.

The hull's sudden groan as he lifts himself up.

He whispers, these things are real, yet you are losing your mind.

He sucks deep upon the leaden air, leans over the boat and breathes the salt air off the sea. He watches and sees ray fish deep down, shadowbirds in slow flight.

Just then Hector puts a hand on Bolivar's shoulder.

He leaps back and screams and drops the knife.

Hector says, relax, Porky.

Bolivar stares at the knife. He stares at Hector's pecked-out eyes watching where the knife might be. Bolivar moves then, grabs the knife, scrambles towards the stern, sits with the knife pointed.

Hector climbs back into the cooler.

He says, really, Porky, you should join me in here. It is hot as hell outside.

During the night Hector begins to call for Bolivar who lies uneasy and cannot sleep. In the dawn, Hector slides out of the cooler and looks towards Bolivar.

He says, there has been plenty of time to think, Porky. There is much to discuss. What type of man you are. You are not as simple as you contend. Surely, Porky, you understand this.

Bolivar presses the blade into the palm of his hand.

An unknown white bird lands upon the trim. Hector leans suddenly forward, the eyes upon the bird as though it can be seen. Bolivar watching the testing black bill. The quick wing-flick as it webs forward onto the deck.

It steps towards the meat resting in a container of sea-water and pecks at it. Then it steps back as though aware by instinct it has met itself. Hector slides the meat towards it, laughs as the bird eats.

There are always choices, isn't that so, Porky? Choices and consequences. One thing leads to another. All men understand this.

Bolivar cannot meet the eyes.

Hector says, what can a man know about himself? It is a difficult matter. Different for every man. In your case,

Porky, you maintain that life is a simple affair. Yet the question of will must always be looked at. How much of the will is the man. How much the man is aware of the will. The path made by the will, whether it is blind or not. In every man this is different. We must think about you, Porky. The will as expressed within you. That time on the beach. Were you aware of what you were doing? The boat you willed out to sea and beyond. Into that storm. Towards my death. You acted without questioning the source of your actions. What was the source? A type of darkness, maybe. An unknown thing inside you. The dark will leading you, Porky, blindly, from one thing to another. The will seeking always more of this and that. You see, Porky, you are not a man but an unthinking thing. An animal, really. A base instinct. An animal in thrall to the instincts. The man you think you are does not in fact exist. That means you, Porky, do not exist. Really, you are nothing. This is simple to understand.

Bolivar sits shut-eyed, holding the blade against the palm of the hand. He can hear the bird pecking at the meat. Hector's quiet laughter.

Bolivar wakes from comfortless sleep. He opens his eyes upon a shut sky, the waters voided, he cannot see a thing. It is then he hears Hector moving outward from the cooler. He grips the knife. Hector's body travelling as though floating in the dark. Then the whispered voice close by.

Are you asleep, Porky? Do you want to know what happened to her? Your child. Shall I tell you?

Get away from me.

✻

In the morning, he is skinning a bird when Hector climbs out of the cooler. The gaunt hand feeling its way across the boat.

Bolivar wheels upon him with the knife.

Did you have a good sleep, Porky?

The space between them hot and airless until a ruffle of wind pulls Hector's hair from his eyes.

Bolivar watching Hector's bloodless face.

Hector watching Bolivar with a fixed blind look.

Bolivar shouts. You have no eyes. The birds ate your eyes. Why are you pretending to see?

Hector shrugs and opens his hands.

He says, blindness is a type of seeing, is it not? Are we not blind when we dream? And yet we see. Sometimes what we see is perfectly clear. The dream reveals what you are afraid to look at. What you are afraid to think. How many people look into the dream for what is real? You never thought to look, Porky. So I am seeing what is real for you, what you cannot allow yourself to see.

I said get away from me.

You abandoned your child, Porky. Your only daughter.

I said leave me alone.

How old was she again? Three or four years old? What is a child at this age?

Bolivar's breathing clots in his mouth. He is afraid to move. Over and over he says to himself, do not listen to the words, his words are lies.

He moves stiffly backward until he is crouched against the hull. Shutting his eyes to a needling light. Pressing the blade into his hand, tasting the blood.

Hector says, the daughter standing in the shadow of the father. Tell me, Porky, who is that man? How is he a man, a father? The figure running away. You can see him, can't you, the shadow in flight. Do you know where she is now? Do you know her tale? The child that never knew your love. I will tell you, Porky. I will tell you what you have sown. When a woman does not know love she abases herself before love. Your daughter became a whore. Yes, she was had by many, many men. She was had by those in the cartel you ran from. They had her like a dog. They swapped her around, one by one, two by two, then they cut her throat and dumped her in the hills. All this is to be expected. You were not there to protect her from this life. It is as they say. Nothing gives to nothing, Porky, don't you think?

Bolivar sits scratching his face. His beard is wet with tears and blood. The cheekbone swollen by blows from his fist. He shakes his head and tells himself, his words are just lies, lies, he cannot know the truth, how can he know the truth? He pulls at his hair and stares into her face. It is drawn of shadows, fleeting and half-seen, a bloodless underwater flower. He whispers the name of his daughter until the sound of her name becomes strange to him. He asks himself, who were you then? What were you? Why did you? What is it you have done? He squeezes his hands in anguish.

He cowers against the hull, the gaunt shadow growing out of the body. A great shaking in his hands. Then a thought arrests him. His head snaps up and he roars, it is not true!

I would have heard! My cousin knows where to find me. No one but he has known.

He lets loose a wild laugh, climbs up and moves with the knife calling for Hector.

You are a liar, he says. I know what you are doing. You are trying to trick me. You want this boat for yourself.

Hector says, your cousin is long dead.

Then he says, be careful with that knife, I cannot see you coming.

Hector begins to climb out of the cooler. Bolivar watching him as he feels his way until he reaches the birds. There are three left among the mess of dead birds, two types of gull and a tern. Then Hector with blind hands quickly wrings each neck. He throws them overboard, then turns upon Bolivar.

It is pointless, Porky, what you are trying to do. You cannot escape. When an act is committed it is written into your life.

Bolivar puts his fingers into his ears.

Hector unfolds his hands and seems to stare at them as though each hand were taking measure of some truth.

Then he shrugs.

He says, what was your mother's name again?

It is then that Bolivar turns and opens his eyes, stares at Hector. He grabs at the knife and begins towards him.

I am warning you. Do not speak of her.

Yes, Estelle. That was her name. You have not spoken much about her, your own mother. It is as if you were trying to forget her also. This is a shame, don't you think? Maybe it is even a crime. The burden a mother must carry.

It is true that each birth wounds the mother because the child is born through the heart. The heart is torn open with love. This is a wound that never heals. But here is the question, Porky. What does the son do for the mother in return? In your case, you closed off your heart. She watched as you abandoned her, Porky. You rejected the mother's love. Yes, it can be said that this is what men do. But you walked out of her life as though it were as simple as closing a door. She asked herself over and over what she did wrong. She began to curse her own womb. She wanted to tear it out, to undo herself of your birth. She never knew what became of you. And when she died, she died without sight of you. Yes, Porky, all this has happened—

Bolivar slowly bends over a low groan, his hands over his ears. She is not dead, she is not dead, he is lying. The scream building within him is savage and black. It resounds then out of the moving body. The hands reaching out as the body comes upon Hector, the hands grabbing Hector by the hair and the throat, the hands that drag the youth across the deck, then hoist Hector up against the trim, the youth screaming, pleading, his hands without power. The sudden cursed shout that leaves Bolivar's mouth as Hector is lifted and thrown into the water. The eyes watching as Hector flails blindly, the hands reaching for something to grip but the mind is without bearing and blind in the sea, the youth turning one way and another, there is nothing to hold on to, he lets loose a scream, he shouts to Bolivar, save me, I can't see—

Then there is silence. The eyes watching the resting water.

*

He lies spent and breathless against the hull. His head hanging. His hands shaking in his lap. He does not want to think. But the mind screams within the body.

Why did you do it? They will know for sure what you did. It will be easy to work out. They will ask, where is he? You will not be able to answer. They will say that you killed him and ate him. How can you prove you did not?

An eye for an eye.

An eye for an eye for an eye. That is how it is. They will find people to kill you.

He sees them ranged before him. He is speaking to them, pleading, their eyes searching his face as he talks.

Look, it was like this. He refused to eat. He starved himself to death. What could I do about it? He had this crazy idea he was next to God. It was the mind gave up first. Then the body followed.

Look, he drowned in the storm. I tried to save him. It happened so quick. It was that storm that took him. The waves were as big as a two-storey house. There was nothing I could do.

A sound reaching from a dream. *Schlik schlik, schlik schlik.* Bolivar wakes from broken sleep and wants to wake again. He blinks upon spreading blood light. His own blood heavy and unwilling, his dry tongue tacked to the roof of his mouth. He sits watching the empty cooler rise out of the shadows. The blindness of wind. The silence of light as it spreads its blood within the boat. The knife resting on his thigh. It is then he sees within the light's unfolding the rows of lines carved into the hull. His breathing stops. His body leans forward.

What he sees is the hull scored with an infinitude of what was scored before. An endless series of barred lines criss-crossing the bodywork. He lets out a wounded roar, his hand fumbling for the knife. He kneels to the hull, begins to scratch out the lines but there are so many now, endless weeks amounting to years, his mind cannot take sight of it all. The knife upon the hull and it is then that he turns and sees Hector standing over him.

He cowers backward and screams.

Hello, Porky.

The heat rests in silence upon the water. Hector sits with a wrinkle of a smile. His hands playing with a dead tern. Blood wets his fingers as it drips onto the deck. His blind-eyed gaze fixed upon Bolivar.

Hector says, I cannot believe it, Porky. You tried to kill me. This makes you a murderer. And not for the first time either. That time in the hills. What you are still running away from. What you refused to discuss. You were complicit then even if you did not do it.

Bolivar tries to speak against the bile building in the throat. The blood slow and heavy into the rising hand. He manages to point a finger.

That is not true.

You watched that time in the hills, didn't you? Maybe you did not do it. Maybe you did. Maybe you thought about what it would be like to do it. You knew, didn't you, who that man was. The man you buried. He worked in your town. You knew him for years. You knew *what* he was. A man. A father. A husband. All the things you could not be. So you took away from him what you could not have for yourself. Isn't that so? Isn't this how it always is? Isn't this why you fled? You cannot escape what you are, Porky. Which is nothing. That is why all this talk is trivial. Nothing gives to nothing. This is how it is. That is why you should kill yourself.

A rain cloud threatens far-off waters then passes out of sight. He looks and sees a corner of water in the barrel. He dips his cup and takes a small drink and spits it out. The water is nothing but piss. A low laugh echoes from the cooler.

Throughout the night Hector remains quiet. All night Bolivar dreams faces and within the eyes of such faces he sees his own shame. He does not want to wake. When he wakes he can sense Hector waiting.

Watching with blind eyes.

I know you are awake.

Bolivar rubs his eyes with his fists.

It is like this, Porky. All your life, you have spoken of freedom. It is your favourite subject in Gabriela's bar. How simple life is. Follow your desires, you say. Follow your loins and your belly. Please tell me if any of this is not true.

Hector leans forward.

Bolivar cannot move.

You do what you please and you call this freedom.
You speak this word as though you understand it. The
mother of your child. You taught her the meaning of
your freedom, didn't you? The woman cursed by man.
The poisoned fruit of the womb. All those other women
you told me about. You ensnared them one by one. And
poor simple Rosa. You ignored her until there were no
women left. Such are the things that make up your life.
The next plate of food. The next beer. The next female
body to lie beside you. What are you, Porky, but wants
and needs? You are just the body talking. The body's endless, insatiable instinct. You are nothing but an expression
of the body. An expression of that instinct. What I mean
to say, Porky, is that if you do not exist, there cannot be
freedom.

Hector falls quiet a moment. Again he speaks.

Even now as you look at me you are thinking about
what you must do to survive. But it is not you who is
doing the thinking. It is not you who dreams all this. There
never was a you. That is the illusion. Only a man who is
free of all claims of the body understands the meaning of
freedom. Only a man who chooses to die rather than to
live, let me tell you, Porky, that man understands freedom.
Whereas you, Porky, have never lived. And even if you had
sought to truly live, it would never have been possible. So
if you want to taste freedom, Porky, let me tell you—

Hector leans forward and whispers.

Free yourself from the body.

Kill yourself.

*

Bolivar sits a broken figure, his hands shaking on his lap. His face very still watching not the day give way to night but some inward night come upon him. He cannot stop crying. He beats himself about the head, the thighs, beats the hull with his fist. This other person who he sees is himself long ago. He shouts at him but his other self does not listen. He is doing what he wants to do and cannot hear. Bolivar watching helpless before every action.

Hector has moved closer to him.

His voice now a whisper.

All this is simple to understand, Porky. What is living but the will in meeting with the will of others. The simple facts of involvement. The gestures and greetings. The words spoken that lead to understanding. The understandings that lead to duties and debts. Such commerce is one of the laws of life. Such things create affection, bonds, devotion, loyalty to others. The blood trafficking in blood. But such is what you do not give, Porky. And in your not giving you never possessed them. All your life you have been like this. Faithless. Inconstant. False. Always in flight, chasing after your will like a dog. You fled the house of your own flesh and blood. You sought the comfort of women. Who did these women lie with? There was nothing there but a body. And so I can tell you this, Porky. The answer to the meaning of your life. Really, it is simple. It is found in what you have not created. People have forgotten you exist. It did not take them long to forget you. They looked out at the sea and blessed themselves. They shrugged a little. Then they got on with their lives. You see, Porky, you have not touched the heart of another. So there can be no grief. You have passed through life without meaning, Porky. The sea does not know you exist. That is why you should kill yourself.

The knife. The knife going into the hand, hand over fist. The fist turning the point of the knife towards himself. He sits within the stark shadow of the body. Watching the knife, watching the shadow grow within the boat. The shadow more true than the man. This is what he thinks. He brings the knife beneath the ribs. Sits like this a long time. The cold crawling his skin. Watching the shadow's increase within the dark until it meets the dark's completeness.

Then a voice from somewhere inside him speaks.

Do not listen. He is trying to kill you so he can have the boat.

He closes his eyes and just sits.

Something slaps the hull beside him. Bolivar quickly opens his eyes. What he sees is a silver bait fish floundering on the deck. He stares at it confused, lifts his head towards the sky and stares at it. Behind him then a tumult upon the water. He turns to see bait fish leaping out of the sea. Two gulls have come down to squawk and flutter. He knows what this is. A shoal in turmoil tormented by sharks, other big fish. He sees the lithe torsions of dolphins. He grabs at the bait fish as they land on the deck and shouts to Hector.

Look! It is a miracle!

Watching Hector's slim hand upon the cooler as he

lifts himself out. The youth feeling his way along the trim. A bait fish leaps into the boat and wriggles by Hector's feet.

Hector sighs. You are still here, Porky.

Yes, but come and look at this.

What is it?

Come closer and I will show you. Look. Fish are flying into the boat. For sure, it is some kind of miracle.

You know I can't see. I am blind thanks to you.

I thought you said you could see.

I can see other things.

Bolivar watching as Hector moves towards him, the youth pulling the hair out of his face. Bolivar feeling the sudden war summoned by the blood. The war surmounting the old torpor.

He says, I have been listening to you, Hector. I have decided you are right.

Hector smiles and folds his hands.

He says, this is how it should be.

It is then that Bolivar grabs Hector by the hair and puts the knife firmly between the youth's ribs. He pulls the knife free and begins to cut at the neck, the youth letting loose a whistle from the torn valve of the throat. Bolivar lets the body drop, bends and continues to cut.

He shouts, there will be no tricking me this time.

An agonised roar escapes his mouth when he throws the head overboard. Then he closes his eyes and dispatches the body. A moment only before the sharks are upon it, the waters foaming with blood.

Bolivar watches and experiences a sudden chill. He

leans out over the water and screams for Hector, reaches
out his hands, begins to beat at his head.

The body and the head of Hector are gone, the blood
dissolved into water.

What have I done? Now it is really murder.

He weeps without tears in his sleep. Wakes tormented
from dreams. Lies within the feeling left by such dreams.
He is a murderer. Again and again, this is what is revealed
to him. That he planned Hector's death, led him to it, not
here on the boat, but back on the strip. A secret thing,
hidden even from himself. He stares at himself as he was
in the dream trying to see who he is.

He lies cowering, confused, not sure which is true,
if he planned to kill Hector back on the strip or if he
planned to kill him here on the boat.

He stares into the dream that rests upon the water.

Either way, he is dead. It was you who killed him.

The moon and the stars are outing wrong. The wind has
been dead for days. The current that carries the panga
slows and then stops altogether.

He thinks, if you do not move, you will not use up
any moisture.

He tries not to suck on his tongue or his teeth.

He thinks his heart is exhausted.

He wakes from another dream wherein they are coming to kill him. He studies the sea with suspicion. He sees
now the boat has swivelled to face the North Star.

Two nights later the boat points south-west.

You are going in circles.
You are going back home.
You are going to hell.

For hours he watches rain smoke the distant waters. His hands fondling the cups. He closes his eyes and can taste water loosening his mouth. The blood cleansed again and flowing into the heart. Little by little he sees what is coming is not rain but fog. It travels serene and without wind as though following the drift of its own thought. The air turns clammy and clings to his skin, beads the hull with moisture. Soon the boat is masked with dew. He pulls off his T-shirt and sucks the wet out of it. Crawls the panga on hands and knees licking the hull. When he looks up he sees with horror that the sea has fallen away.

He is falling out of time. This is what he thinks. He cannot be sure how many days he has spent in this fog lying crooked in the cooler, his chin touching his knees, his mouth sucking moisture from his clothes. His mind tasting clear water. Water bundled over rocks. Water splashing into his cup. He cannot remember how long it was since he last crawled the hull.

He lifts his eyes and listens to the small echoings in the fog as though sound itself is coming undone.

Then he sits up.

He has heard voices. People murmuring close by.

He listens carefully.

This cannot be true, he thinks.

His voice sounds out fearful and unsure.

Who's there?

He listens.

A woman whispers but not to him.

He is afraid to ask who it is.

Then his hand grips the cooler. They are talking about him.

Yes, it is true, the woman's voice says. He was a bad son. But he was like all sons, guilty of being born a man. You carry him inside you—

Mama—

You nurse him and you carry him in your arms. You do this and that for him – all the things a mother does, you are tormented day and night, you go without, you get no thanks whatsoever. But you never think that some day he will abandon you. That one day you will wake up and he will be gone. I did not know until now he was a murderer. Maybe he was always such. For sure there is a part of me he has killed. I did not bring him up to be like this. I did not bring him up to make life more difficult for everyone else. Maybe he is a murderer, who knows what a man is capable of. But he is dead to me, my own son. To think all that time I was carrying something dead in my belly—

Bolivar lies clutching his hair and weeping dry tears. He squirms and wraps his arms about his knees. He calls out in a hoarse voice but she does not hear him, she is busy talking to somebody else.

Then he hears the voice of another.

He tries to call out with a swollen tongue.

Papa. What are you doing here? How did you find me?

He is punishing us. Maybe he is punishing us for sins in some past life, who knows. Maybe he is not of our blood. I've heard of such things. A bastard switched at birth. That would make sense to me, for sure. Look how many are born around here. It would have been easy. How can I believe he is my own son? Look at him. He is not in my image. I will admit he called me once to tell me he was safe. But I did not tell you this for fear of the pain it would cause you. I would say to you, look, he will be fine, you will hear from him when this trouble he has caused dies down. For sure, I could not tell his wife, his daughter. After a while I could see he was living another life somewhere else, who knows where he was. No doubt he had met another woman. Such is always the case. I did not bring him up to be like this. What I want to know is, how could he be my son?

He wishes he had more tears to wring this pain out through the crying eyes. There is no more fluid left in the body. His gut seized with cramps. He imagines the knife searching the veins of his wrist. The tip loosening from the flesh a runnel of blood. The lips reddening as he drinks life from the skin.

He is woken by voices. Does not know for how long he has slept. He knows they are still speaking about him.

Then he says, please, I am dying, bring me water.

The fog is beginning to thin here and there to reveal the cold tar sea.

Maybe they are on a boat searching for you, he thinks. Maybe they are lost also.

A seabird alights upon the trim. He screws his eyes at the bird as it jigs about the deck.

Then she is speaking again to somebody else. He hears the other voice and cowers back into the cooler, begins to pull at his hair.

He whispers, Alexa, please, no. I do not want to hear.

How could I know him? she says. He is there only as a ghost, a shadow within me. I think of him almost never. Sometimes I dream about him and he is there as a feeling, but when I call to him he walks away. Maybe I am searching for him in other men. It is not a question of forgiveness. The sin is ancient. It originated before my time. That is what I reckon. It is as you say. He was born into nature. He is guilty of being born a man. All men are like this, or maybe not all of them. Many perhaps. Maybe there is a choice. It is not for me to say.

He is not my son.

God is the father of the devil but the devil is the father of man. That is what I always say. He is made in the devil's image for sure.

He is not my father. I look nothing like him.

His own voice whispering, over and over.

Man is the father of the devil.

The father is the devil in man.

What man ever looks the same way twice when you look at him? Even my own husband. You will find no truth in a man. If he is a murderer he deserves whatever will happen to him. I wash my hands. You cannot expect a mother to put up with everything.

They asked me to decide whether he is guilty or not.

Who asked you?

He must be guilty. He willed his own fate, did he not?
He made all this happen.

Well then, he will die alone. He cut all ties with the
world.

Hell is nothing but shame. Soon he will find this out.
That will be his fate. He will be his own judge.

He can hear the soft cuffing of the bird's feet. He
is thinking of the vein in its neck. Suddenly he surges
towards the bird, his hands outreached, his hands arriving
upon nothing.

It is raining in the dark when he wakes. The panga rising
and falling upon a swell. He crawls near-blind and weak-
ened out of the cooler, feeling for the cups. He falls onto
his back and drinks, the water sliding over the swollen
tongue, the cold rain striking the face and alerting the
skin. He opens his eyes and it is then he sees the fog
is gone. He sups water until he is drunk, the moon an
impossible fruit.

For days it rains without cease. He is coming to be
again. This is what he feels. The mouth living at the
edge of the cup. The mind feeling the water go to work
within the body. He can almost see it, the water sluicing
the blood, the blood rinsing clean the heart. The mind
renewing in the body.

He thinks he was beset by a dream brought on by drought in the body. And yet the dream lives within him as though real. He hears himself whisper. They will not— Why would they? Why would they come? They will leave me to this punishment. The rain upon this nothing sea. This nothing sea reaching without end. The end never reached. You held within the nothing. It is a strange and lonely fact that you exist.

He puts his hand to his heart.

And yet your heart beats. It beats as though you were not nothing. This beating heart feels.

He sits clutching at his arms, his mind gripped by loneliness.

He is sitting against the hull when he discovers it. If he does not move nor open his eyes he can see her as she sits. His hands very still as he watches. She is getting up from the chair. Her hands upon the arms of the chair and turning. He tries to look. Her face turning into light. He sits squeezing his eyes and tries to see. She is getting up from the small bamboo chair and turning. She is standing up from the chair and turning the chair in another direction. In her turning he can see the curl of her almond hair as it rests upon her shoulder. A red cardigan. Almost her eyes. He stares and holds his breath. She is getting up from the chair and she is turning the chair and she shrugs, pouts her lips, she is looking at him. Almost her face. He tries to see her face but the mind cannot hold a clear image, the image briefly seen cannot be held twice. She is looking at him and he can see her mouth as she speaks. *I don't want to.*

This is what she says. He has asked her a question. He does not open his eyes. He does not breathe. He does not know what he has asked her. She is getting up off the chair, she is fed up, she is turning the chair into the light, the same light that falls upon her almond hair, the blushed cheek. Then he sees her hands rise up in a protest of some kind. Almost her eyes. *I don't want to.* This is what she says. This is what she *did*. He remembers the moment from so long ago as he looks at it but he cannot remember what surrounds it. What he was doing. What he did after this. What it was he asked her. For a long time he does not move. *I don't want to.* Almost her face. How memory sees with feeling not seeing. What he sees is the feeling of a face. Now he is with her. He is helping her move the chair. Then he is picking her up. He is touching her skin. He presses his finger gently into her cheek and feels the run of her teeth. He strokes her hair, separates the strands with his fingertips. He sits a long time like this, his eyes squeezed shut, barely breathing. When he does not breathe he can feel the tiny breath in her chest. He can hold her like this. He puts his arms around her and he is able to speak into her ear. Skin to skin. Almost her eyes.

He whispers, I was gone.

I was gone but a great storm blew me back to you.

The moon black-born while Hector was alive is waning towards its end. He can feel the water's rising sap within the body, begins to pace the deck. Stands willing for some doing thing. His sight absorbed by emptiness. Now and again he can see some refuse. An item that looks like polystyrene. Then a pandemonium of shearwaters.

He wakes with a sense of something nearby. His eyes combing the half-light. Then he sees some plastic bags floating within reach of the bow. He wonders how he could have heard this. He takes the plank and draws them in, carefully unknots the first bag. What he sees is some medical waste. Discoloured gauze. Cuttings of what might be blood-stained fabric. Something else that causes him to close the bag and retch. He throws the bag overboard. Then slowly he examines the second bag. He unties it to see four plastic bottles with faded labels. Each contains about a cup of brown fluid. He takes a suspicious sniff, tips a finger into the fluid and allows a small taste. It is industrial, somewhat alcoholic, strangely resinous and forbidding. He puts it to his lips and takes a small drink and it comes upon him quick, a sudden feeling of lucidity and strength. The fluid rushing the blood, he can feel it in his hands and legs. He wants to row the boat ashore. He wants to swim towards home. He stands up and shouts and moves about with renewed energy. Later, he sits and stares at the bottles. He does not care what this fluid is. He pours a small drop into a cup and calls it coffee, thins it out with water.

When he wakes each day he reaches over the trim. The sun within its pale increase. His hand scooping the cold sea. He washes his face, his hands, then he bathes the sores on his skin with brine. He dries with a yellow rag that he hangs with a discoloured peg.

He puts on a pair of shorts, a T-shirt and Hector's sweater, which now fits him. He makes coffee but does not eat. He reads whatever he can find. A book belonging to his father or a newspaper he can recall. He stares at photos in the newspaper of people from back home. Their images forming and reforming in a dreamlike and fluid consortium.

He sits and feels the nodding green of the palm trees. The sunlight upon the beach. The bright green fronds shadow-laid in grey-green along the edges of the strip. He thinks of the bodies passing. The motion of walking. The hands languid, the shoulders circular in motion, the toes curling as the feet print the sand. The mouths supple and wet-licked while talking. He thinks about what it is to walk freely, easily. To go from one place to another. How each body moves in a thoughtless echo of all such bodies moving within such daily orbits.

He takes long walks around the cooler. His feet following the road over the crumbling bridge. Past the beachside cabanas full now with tourists. Burning diesel that drifts from a pickup truck. The air sawing where Memo is running tests on an outboard motor. He steps past men in T-shirts rank with sweat and fish and beer. Leans into the fragrance of guava leaves smoking on charcoal. The waft of cooking fish.

He studies the outness of the world. The profound colours of night. His ear attending to the silence. A growing feeling of awareness coming upon him. What you are among this. He imagines an ocean full of container ships and tankers, each ship moving constant and true and yet all passing within this same silence, the silence itself passing within this outness that is itself always silent. He studies the panga as it rides the swell. His body as it sits in the boat. He examines the feeling of being adrift within this outness until he can no longer measure himself.

And yet you are here.

He thinks about this and cannot understand it.

He thinks of the different ways he could meet death. A swallowing wave. A sudden storm. Hunger setting the body adrift. Thirst setting the mind adrift from the body. And yet he knows he is going to live. It is a feeling that sits alive within him. He tries to examine this feeling but cannot explain it to himself.

He asks, but how can you know? Where can such a feeling come from?

He thinks, perhaps it is a question of probability, of doing the right things. There are birds to eat. Fish if you are lucky. There is water in the barrel. You do this and that and you keep your head screwed on and maybe you survive.

He watches the dark washed by the moon.

Gazes upon a distant star fallen upon the water.

Knows it for the jewelled light of a ship.

Always now she is with him and he sees her both as a child and young woman. She sits at the verge of his sight. She sits in the bamboo chair and giggles. She is older, studying a book. She is applying lipstick, putting on a coat. He tells her about the many things he is doing. He says, you will not believe it, but I have grown old and am returning home a different man. All this is thanks to you. You must walk down a path before you are able to return. Isn't that always so?

His mind running over the different things he will say to her. He can see himself humble before her door. Then sitting before her, his head bowed, his hands folded on his lap. Afraid to look her in the eyes.

I did not offer you the comfort of a father.

I did not give comfort to others.

I understand this now.

Then he shrugs, hears himself mutter, maybe I was not to blame. He thinks about this. Maybe a man is not to be blamed if he has not yet been confronted by truth. Who is to know the how and the when of a man encountering his truth? How long this journey takes. What matters is that he encounters it.

Over three days he catches four birds and puts them in the aviary. He runs daily around the cooler, pushing through the fatigue, feeling the creak in his joints. He thinks, for sure, you have aged a bit. Maybe ten years or so, maybe more. He tongues at a hole in his gum where a molar fell out and he cannot remember it happening. His nails are yellowing and wrinkled. His hands not the thick hands he has known. The wrists are thin. The shoulders gone to bone.

He stares at the sea hoping to see himself.

A half-seen stranger with long hair stares back. The face fowled and hidden under beard.

He shakes his head at this substitute watching in the water. Raises a hand and the substitute's hand mirrors his own. He opens his mouth and shouts and the mouth before him opens. He turns then but senses in the moment of turning his double remaining on the water unmoved.

He leans over the trim and stares hard at the water.

*

These are days of distant lightning, pulses of light in a hundred-mile sky. He feels an ancient awe. A sense of great chaos beyond reach. He wakes into the faint reek of sulphur. Can see in the dim light the panga has crossed the wake of a ship. Discoloured waste upon the water. The who of them. What has passed into nothing.

Then comes a quickening swell of water marble-topped. He pours coffee and goes to sit in the cooler, gets up and checks the water barrel. He takes a long inhale of air. The sky smells different. Rain will fall and stay down for days.

With careful strokes he cuts up chicken and places it in brine, puts it in the cooler. He unties his growing hoard of plastic bags and sorts through them. There are bags in every colour and script. He studies the bleached logos, the unknown languages. Smudged words and ideograms. For a moment he can see himself as though in some final days of man, puzzling upon these plastic bags as the remnants of lost and distant races, all such writing patiently washed to nothing by the sea. He takes a long clear plastic bag and puts it over his head, tears a hole for his mouth. Then he takes it off and puts on all the clothing he has left – two pairs of shorts, two T-shirts, two sweaters and his hat.

Waiting for what comes.

The wind harries the plastic sheeting and forces the rain inside. He has been damp through for days. His teeth clacking an arrhythmic beat. He thinks, your bones will turn to putty. He climbs out into the rain and holds the plastic bag with one hand to his body. Begins to run at walking speed raising high his knees. He flexes his jaw as he moves, pumps his free hand into a fist, beats his chest. On his third circuit he slips and the sea vaults the lowered sky. He finds himself winded on his back, pain throbbing in his hip. He lies clutching at his side and is afraid to move. He stares at the vanished sun, the ceaseless rain, how the rain seems to have given time a shape, time slowly wet and lumbering and visible just for a moment. He crawls to the cooler and does not know why he is laughing.

He wakes upon a wild and running sea, grabs at his hip. He crawls wincing towards the cups, gathers them into a plastic bag and ties it upon a hook. He grabs hold of the seat and lifts himself up. Stands eyeing the sea, the clotted heavy light spreading downward. Soon, the temperature drops and it begins to hail. Then his skin begins to tingle, his hair rising up. He tries to move quickly to the cooler but a staff of lightning strikes the ocean before him. He yelps, crawls inside with the flash still imprinted on his eye. Trying to fit his body upon the bed of polystyrene foam without touching the cooler.

For days the raving sea. In the dark the rain falls as though into some timeless abyss. He becomes aware of the sensation of parting from his body. He closes his eyes and watches as if he is becoming someone else. He is sitting on the seat watching the lightning strike the sea, then he turns and sees himself in the cooler. He discovers if he holds his breath he can rise high into the storm. High above the sea he can see the panga a dim-thrown speck, the moon tossed upon the ocean.

When the storm abates, he can hardly move. A furious exhaustion rips through the upper body. He lies coughing wet from his lungs, his bailing arms limp. How the storm still presses in memory the dark and shrieking shape of a mouth. Watching the shadows where Alexa sits. He says, I am still here because of you. He watches the dawn blood the world. The barrel now a quarter full. He takes a long drink and washes the salt off his face. He drinks some coffee and sees that in a few more days it will be gone. He cannot go for a run, can hardly walk for his hip. He climbs back into the cooler and waits.

He sits staring into the well of his being. Can feel something within him move, the living will restless to escape, a shadow coming loose. At night and sometimes during the day he begins to part from his body. He comes to believe he is double. Sometimes he wakes with the empty feeling he is someplace else. He fixes his mind upon this problem of separation until he grows tired. What it would be like to separate for good, to gain control of his double, to leave the other behind for good.

He visits where he used to live. His breathing held as he stands within the shadows. The brass-handled door opens with a faint rasp as he soft-foots into her room. The night-breathing window. His daughter asleep. The hair spread darkly upon the pillow.

The sea her breathing.

Then she turns abruptly as though wakened. She stares at the dark as though she can see him. She sighs and mutters some misshapen word.

What he whispers into her ear.

She turns and falls back asleep.

Maybe, he thinks, this is how it is. You are really in this room watching over her and in some way she senses it. This would explain a lot of things.

He visits the house of his parents. Steps over the sleeping hound old and deaf in the doorway. Meets their slumped and sleeping bodies. His mother's face held gaunt by the street light when he leans in to examine her. The familiar smells. Decongestant. Detergent on the mopped floors. Candle wax.

He visits places he has never been. He imagines cities vast, teeming, met with festival colour. Faces like painted masks looming as he walks down the streets. He ghosts into different rooms. Sits watching people eat, people watching TV while eating, gaping into phones.

He enters a room and stands with men and roars at a football match. He steps into another room and watches an enormous man bent over a woman.

He inhales cigar smoke, damp newspapers, cinder, oranges in a box. He peels an orange and puts it to his nose. He sniffs scorched chilli, epazote, squeezes a lime on his tongue. He walks into a bakery and breathes in the smell of shortbread. He crumbles some and lets it drop upon the floor.

He places before him foods he has never dreamed of. Obscure meats and pickles. For fun he licks garlic, salt, pepper, mustard, a meat garnish that tastes of chocolate. He sucks on sugared chilli.

Each night he visits with women.

Debris washes against the boat. He pulls some in and sorts through it. Plastic bags and bottles. Seaweed streamers. Knots of netting shredded beyond use. He examines an empty crisp bag. Fondles a fly swat and tries to picture its owner. He cuts open a shampoo bottle and pours some seawater in, lathers the shampoo into his scalp. His hair now is long and knotted. Then he remembers a broken comb Hector once found and searches for it. He finds it in a plastic bag, begins to detangle his hair, runs the comb through the matting of beard.

Later that evening he visits Rosa's house. A gentle listening knock before she opens the door. She stands in

the half-light and with a flick lets down her hair. Her
eyes cannot hide her alarm at the sight of his body. She
touches his meatless arm and gasps. Her hand tracing the
ribs. She slides out of her loose shirt, his hand upon her
abdomen.

He says, I am sorry, Rosa, I haven't had time to shave.

Afterwards, his body spent, he lies overcome with the
feeling that his double has always existed.

He says to Rosa, if I can become him, I will be able to
leave the boat for good. It is only a matter of concentra-
tion. Then I will be free to do what I like. This other me
I can leave behind for good.

Rosa runs her finger along his chest.

She says, what happens to him will be of no concern
to me.

Under a blank sky he idles with the knife. It is then he
stops and listens. He quickly cuts at bird claws and feathers and throws them overboard. He leans over the trim
and watches, listens for a long time.

The sheer sea deepening into darker colours.

He believes his hearing.

He strips off his clothes and puts the knife in his mouth
tasting the blade. He takes a small web of netting. With a
light gasp he eases his body into the water. He is afraid to
let go of the boat. He treads the water then takes a long
breath and slides under the panga. The ocean below a vast
dusk upturned, the water burning his eyes. He can see no

sharks. He watches glimmering transports of colour. He grows emboldened and swims under the boat. The hull has taken the countenance of rock, dark and rugged and sharpened by barnacles.

He takes the knife from his mouth and goes to work.

He arranges the catch before him as though on a plate. Picks up a barnacle and pinches it free of its sleeve. A spout of brine squirts him in the face. He wipes at his cheek and laughs. With slippy fingers he pulls each barnacle out of its skin and studies it. How each snail-like body looks like a reptilian foot. He takes a pinch of brine from a cup and seasons the meal. He becomes his tongue, his mind singing the flesh as he eats. He decides the barnacles taste entirely of the sea. He wonders too if he is now like this. If now you are made of wind and rain, salty air, the blood watered to brine. How you might taste to a shark.

Later, he lies on his back, resting his hands on his ribs. His mind adrift and for a moment he is met with a sense of all life within the ocean. He follows the thought and stops before an untold immensity. All that has ever lived within the seas. His mind trying to reach. The time that has held all such life. The time passing. The time that will pass onwards and forever. He can imagine all the fish beneath him now. All the fish in all the world's seas. All the fish going back in untold generation. Each fish a being, the being within the body, the body with a sense of feeling that is its own aliveness, this aliveness living briefly and then vanishing into a void of years.

What you are in all this.

He turns to the form that is Alexa sitting beside him.

He says, do you know what? Man gives birth to his own problems. I see this now. The world has always been silent.

Days pass and he sleeps more during the day. He catches sight of his double in dream but more often now he cannot become him, the double is slipping away. His water is low and he rests each drop in the eaves of his mouth. For days and days he pulls at the sky with his eyes, pulls at it as though unrolling some great scroll, unrolling until he finds rain. He imagines growing tall enough to tear at the sky, ripping it to shreds with his hands, the fabric of the world coming undone. He wonders what would be behind it. Space. Blackness. A giant echo of laughter. He sits and sucks on his tongue. The coffee is gone. Soon, he thinks, you will have to start drinking bird blood.

He sits at the stern willing himself under a colding sky. He can see himself under the boat. The jabbing knife. He is filling the small net with barnacles. The will sending forth the image of the will to do the will's bidding. How the will presses against the feeling that says, today, the waters are not quiet.

No, he says. I will not do it.

He finds himself moving, taking breath upon the knife, sliding silently into the cool water. In an instant he knows his weakness. How the water's irrevocable weight binds him, pulls him down, whispers stop to the limbs. His eyes searching the fathomless gloom. He sees the passing carriage of minute yellow-dark fish. Then he sees the will's work as though watching his double. Slowly he brings himself under the boat. Chipping at the hull while counting the breath. Lost in the work when out of the dusk curves a sickle-tailed shark. His breath flees and the hand opens letting the knife drop into the sea's falling dark.

The sun undone upon the sea.

He finds himself breaking the surface, grabbing hold of the gunwale, hauling himself into the boat, coughing up water. He lies very still, waiting for the blood to warm, lying in grief for his knife.

The last bird in the boat, a shearwater, carried the speckled rain in its feathers. Now he talks to it a while. He asks it for forgiveness.

He wonders if he is on the edge of a shipping lane. In four days he has watched two great ships edge the horizon. Seen the lights of another at night. He wonders who they are, what they are doing. He closes his eyes and sits at the officers' table. He dances with their wives. He takes hold of a woman and hears her gasp, begins to waltz her about the deck. A rich laughter falls out of him. It is Rosa.

His arms beat against the cold. Watching how fire lives on water as the illusion of fire.

He dreams of who she is now, her form as she moves within him, a woman soon, moving through the world, his form moving within her, unseen, unknown. He sings to her at night in a hoarse low voice. Sometimes she speaks to him. You must survive, she says. You must return home. I know you will.

He laughs a little, says, I am doing what I can but it is getting harder and harder all the time. I am weak and very hungry now. My body is tired. Look at this. My arms are like sticks. I have not caught a bird in some time.

*

Paul Lynch

He lies watching her move. He watches the forms of others he has known as they move through their lives. He stands on the street or in the room watching. He thinks he might be a ghost. The motions of the living. This is what he sees now. How each person moves burdened within time yet time moving without. How each moves through life in pain and fright, in suffering and bewilderment, feeling through the darkness, their hands grasping like the blind for there is no real seeing. He closes his eyes and breathes softly and feels a spreading light within. He sees them all before him, those that he knew.

He is crying.

He knows now that he loves them all. He sees his younger self and loves him too.

A strange feeling of bliss.

Without sight he can sense a lone bird far off. He turns to see a chevron of falling light. The bird plunging into the sea. He stands up and calls, waves with a plastic bag.

Little by little he becomes aware of it. A deep quiet in the mind. For a long time it has been so, the days passing in silence. But now when he wakes his mind is still. No more the bullying voice he has heard all his life. He cannot explain this to himself. Without thought, he sits.

Storm.

From bottomless sleep he is startled awake. He meets a fierce and blinding light. He pushes back the plastic sheet and visors his hand over his eyes. From upon the night sea a torch beam is directed upon the boat. He can hear low voices, the rumbling of an engine that reverberates through the hull of the panga. He sees the light of a cigarette moving in brief hand arcs.

This is happening, he thinks. This is not a dream.

With disbelief his body is moving out of the cooler. He waves his arms and shouts with furious hoarseness. What he sees is a short but powerful cruiser sheathed by the dark, not a single light on board, its outline faint by moonlight. The shapes of three men. He continues to shout as the light travels down the length of the panga then fixes back on his body.

A man shouts in a foreign tongue.

He hears another voice, high and urgent, and he thinks it might be Japanese but he has no idea why. The beamed light goes black and the vessel becomes complete with the darkness. He watches a cigarette brighten as it is sucked and then the butt is flicked towards him, lands by his feet.

The cruiser engine is throttled into a roar.

His mouth goes dry. He cannot shout.

The boat powering away.

He lies on the deck heaving great sobs, sucks the dying cigarette. He tells himself, perhaps it is the case you are only ever met with one chance. There are no other chances. This was your chance and you let it go. He wonders if this is true. He wonders what he could have done. Jumped overboard. Swum towards the boat.

A feeling of something black creeping under the skin, the black seizing tight around the heart.

The moon rounding upon quarter-light.

He rolls and begins to punch the hull, breaks open a knuckle.

It was real, you saw it.

He stands up and stares at the dark.

He roars at the sea. Goddamn you! Why could you not leave me alone?

When he wakes in the morning he sits and wonders if what happened during the night was true. He cannot tell for sure. He can see the boat as it was in darkness upon the water, no masthead light, side light or stern light. Criminals no doubt, pirates or traffickers, and yet, when he thinks about it, he cannot be sure what it truly was. He looks for the cigarette butt and cannot find it. He sits on the stern seat and hears his hoarse voice laughing.

Time empties out of the body. His mind resting again in silence. Hunger now is at its deepest and yet he sits beyond it. Then it rains from a white sky and he is thankful. He measures two fingers of water in the barrel. He studies the chalk face of the moon and speaks to it as an old friend. The moon rising again upon its lustre. He counts how many cycles have gone by and is astonished. It is eleven months since he left home.

Sometimes he sits and simply watches the body as if he has never seen it before. He sees the old hands, the blemished skin, the raw-boned fingers, the crinkled nails, the gaunt ankles and feet. There is an ache that is always present. The slow heavy blood has stiffened the limbs, brought short the breath. He no longer has the energy to run. How suddenly youth is old age, he thinks. Now you are an old man.

All day now he sits in the cooler or on the deck, his mind present with the water, his mind present with the sky and the wind, he is both within and without them.

He feels as though the great silence has entered the body, is running through the blood, quietening the heart's longings.

He listens to the silence and it meets him as feeling.

He wonders if the same silence he can feel within is the same silence of the deep. The silence within the silence. The silence behind all things. He does not know what this means. His mind begins to rest in the feeling of the thought until it cannot be reached.

He becomes aware that he has not heard this silence before.

He can see now how he has been afraid of this silence all his life without knowing it. And now that he can feel it he is no longer afraid. He tries to put form upon the silence. He tries to think of it as sound but it cannot be heard. He tries to think of it as colour. Gradually his mind rests upon the feeling of what silence might mean.

The silence of the past.

The silence of the future.

The silence of the dead.

The silence of those not yet born.

This silence waiting within all living things.

Night will fall upon your journey.

He can see this now and is no longer afraid.

What this silence tells him.

That silence is a form of forgiveness.

He arches his old foot and rubs at the cramp down the length of his calf with wrinkled fingers. Then he sits and seeks within memory. How life used to be on the strip. He can feel inside the memory until feeling is the doing thing. Getting ready now to leave. He opens the cabin door to let in more light upon the mirror. He washes his face in the enamel sink and brushes his stained teeth, takes a toothpick from the box. He wets his cheeks with cologne. Slicks back his hair with cream. He buttons his good black shirt. Then he watches himself in the mirror. He tries to see who he is. He looks carefully until he can see himself as he always was, the hair a little mussed, the skin with its leathery sheen, the bones broad beneath the skin. That big strong body.

You look good, Bolivar. You really do. So this is how it is. This is who you were.

A bird enters the deep white quiet. It lands with a scratch beside him. He studies it with a half-open eye. The bird unknown to him, the feathers black, a beak of fiery crimson. A ringed gaze that meets his own gaze without alarm. Its claws are caught in a mess of discoloured twine. He considers the bird for a moment. He has not the strength to move. And yet the will finds spark within the body, lights through the blood. He finds his fingers upon the twine, the bird taking flight to find it cannot escape. He sits a moment winding the twine while the bird assails his hand with its beak.

His eyes prizing the bird's aliveness.

He licks the blood off his skin.

He says, look, I am sorry, but what do you expect? It is a simple question of laws that already exist. It is either you or me.

For days he drinks water thickened with blood, feeds slowly upon the meat. His body a crooked old thing and yet he can feel the return of some basic strength.

He asks himself if he wants this.

Night is falling upon the ocean. He watches the plunging sun, a burning orange that reaches towards the boat as though lighting a path just for him. His eyes watching the light fall into its deeper hues, the dark smoothing the sea into its oiled night-colours, the sea and the sky vanishing as though into a single becoming. It is then he sees it, the exact moment it happens, the last moment of light upon the water as it meets the dark. He cannot believe it. It is silent. At last, he thinks. You have witnessed this. You always knew it would happen. He can feel it rising through the centre of his being, spreading through his limbs, a tingling whitely of bliss.

By night, by day, he rests within sleep.

He is woken from a dream. He sits up. He has dreamed a different sound in the wavelets as they strike the boat. He moves slowly to the trim and cocks his head and listens to the water. He cannot be sure, it is hard to tell, so he just sits and listens a long time. Then he is sure. He wonders how it can be. And yet it is. There is a different feeling in the water. A feeling of something else.

He sits leaning forward, watching the water release against the boat. He studies the dawn's sedate eruption. Within his body now he can trace the edge of a limit that is a profound and total exhaustion. And yet he wills the will, wills sight to watch the water for this feeling of something else. Evening falls and he is afraid to sleep. He wills himself throughout the night listening to the water, sensing this feeling in the water as though the water's expression can speak. Willing himself into the dawn, listening, watching, feeling the water. Later, he stands slowly up and moves towards the cooler. It is then that he sees it. Serene upon the water. A palm frond floating by. He cannot reach it.

He becomes the feeling carried by the water. He cannot explain it. He studies how the ocean moves and cannot see any difference within it. And yet he feels. Then he sees green and brown. Upon the water two palm fronds pass like hands entwined. With the plank he is able to reach and take hold of one, runs his fingers along the dried-out curling fronds. He puts his nose to it, sniffs hidden within it the old living green. He asks Alexa, what do you think?

✽

He sits defying the midday sun with a sweater over his head. His shadow as it rests is his narrowest self. He sits seeing the water. There is a change now within the current, this much is true. The panga moving freely, yet there is no sign of a swell. His eyes reaching, hoping to reach. And then almost imperceptibly he sees. He does not want to believe. Something is touching the far surface of ocean. He stands on the seat and stares. He rests within his breathing and watches it grow. The blood surging now into the heart. He is afraid to blink.

A veiled and distant shape.

He hears a voice, the old voice within him that speaks. Look, Bolivar. It is a trick of the light. A mirage that looks like an island. How many times has this happened? Or a giant whale. Maybe some floating rubbish catching the sun. Maybe some type of pollution. Who knows what it is. Maybe you are hallucinating again. Do not get your hopes up. Hey! Are you listening to me? Hey!

He stands alert for many hours. His shallow breath hardly meeting the air. What he sees is something massing out of the water. He begins to think it is an island. He is afraid to move in case what he sees might disappear. Then he closes his eyes and opens them. It is still there. He closes his eyes and turns around to face the cooler and opens his eyes upon the encircling sea. Then he turns again and sees what he sees as though it were painted. A rising of grey. A whispering green.

*

It is an island. His mind reeling, his mind still in doubt and yet he knows it for sure. He can feel different energies coursing through him, a moment of sadness met with elation and then he is sad again. He does not know what is wrong with him. The current is carrying the panga towards the shore. You must be dreaming but if you are dreaming this shore looks real. He looks for boats but there aren't any. He looks upon the blurred landscape for buildings or smoke. He wonders now if he is heading towards some uninhabited landscape, what that might mean, another beginning not an ending, he does not care. Hour upon hour the panga drifts until in the afternoon he decides he is close enough to the shore to swim. He sees rocks and a thin-lipped beach. Nodding green trees upon a hill. His mind now fully entering the body, the will entering the blood at full swim. The blood flowing through the heart and into the limbs. He listens to what the limbs tell him, that he has not the strength to swim, that his body is broken, that he is an old man, that he will die in the water. He sits and thinks about this.

He enters the water gripping the trim. For a long time he is afraid to let go. He asks the body to live again. He asks the body to go home. He does not notice he is crying. He still cannot let go.

He makes a slow and heavy forward stroke. The body shouts but obeys. Soon he is without breath, the arms and legs pulling him down and yet he continues forward, his eyes fixed upon the beach. He watches the palm trees upon the beach. The sea, he thinks, there is only the sea and maybe this is only a dream and yet you can feel – the water, the air, the body swims, you are really moving towards the shore, you are going to go home. The heart shouts for blood and he swallows water yet still he is willing the body until he can will it no more. His legs drop and his feet touch rock. Water in the mouth and nose and he is blind for a moment, his arms grappling, and it is then that he falls upon the shore.

He finds himself crawling.

He thinks he can see a haze of smoke. The outline of a hut. He tries to shout but his breath is gone, his voice broken. He can hardly breathe. The feeling of time coming to be again, time flowing into the body, time flowing through thought. This the solid shore. This the solid earth. And then he hears a call. A shadow half-seen becomes a shape moving towards him. He tries to shout. He falls down. The countenance of a child growing before him as he crawls along the beach, his cry broken, he has not the breath to speak, to put into words, he wants to say it over and over again, home, I can go home now, but the words will not come. He falls before the child, it is a little girl, and he lifts his head and he thinks, you believed. A feeling now of the world he once knew. And it is then he finds the breath to speak, and he seeks not to frighten her, speaks in his own tongue.

I am only a fisherman.

A Note About the Author

Paul Lynch is the author of the novels *Red Sky in Morning, The Black Snow,* and *Grace.* He won the Kerry Group Irish Novel of the Year in 2018 for *Grace,* which was short-listed for the Walter Scott Prize for Historical Fiction and the William Saroyan International Prize for Writing the same year. *Grace* was also short-listed for France's Prix Littérature Monde, the Prix Jean Monnet de Littérature Européenne, and *Madame Figaro*'s 2019 Grand Prix de l'Héroïne. *The Black Snow* won France's Prix Libr'à Nous for best foreign novel, and *Red Sky in Morning* was a finalist for the Prix du Meilleur Livre Étranger (Best Foreign Book Prize). He lives in Dublin with his wife and two children.